"Who put you in charge of my life?"

"You did, the second you stepped onto this reserve."

Ouch.

She couldn't argue. She knew that, regardless of her own choices or actions, Joe Peterson felt responsible for her as long as she was on his turf. He was more than ready and willing to "take care of things," as he'd put it.

And in the end, that was what she feared most of all.

That was why she hadn't told him about the other incidents, or about the man in the dark clothes she'd glimpsed near the train two days ago.

Joe's rugged good looks, the obvious physical attraction between them, his strength of character, the concern he tried, but failed, to mask behind that stony expression of his...all of it, taken together, set off cautionary alarms inside her.

It would be far too easy to lean on a man like him, to let him take over, make her decisions, solve her problems for her. But she'd done that once already, and with disastrous results....

Dear Reader,

A new year has begun, so why not celebrate with six exciting new titles from Silhouette Intimate Moments? *What a Man's Gotta Do* is the newest from Karen Templeton, reuniting the one-time good girl, now a single mom, with the former bad boy who always made her heart pound, even though he never once sent a smile her way. Until now.

Kylie Brant introduces THE TREMAINE TRADITION with *Alias Smith and Jones,* an exciting novel about two people hiding everything about themselves—except the way they feel about each other. There's still TROUBLE IN EDEN in Virginia Kantra's *All a Man Can Ask,* in which an undercover assignment leads (predictably) to danger and (*un*predictably) to love. By now you know that the WINGMEN WARRIORS flash means you're about to experience top-notch military romance, courtesy of Catherine Mann. *Under Siege,* a marriage-of-inconvenience tale, won't disappoint. Who wouldn't like *A Kiss in the Dark* from a handsome hero? So run—don't walk—to pick up the book of the same name by rising star Jenna Mills. Finally, enjoy the winter chill—and the cozy cuddling that drives it away—in *Northern Exposure,* by Debra Lee Brown, who sends her heroine to Alaska to find love.

And, of course, we'll be back next month with six more of the best and most exciting romances around, so be sure not to miss a single one.

Enjoy!

Leslie J. Wainger
Executive Senior Editor

Please address questions and book requests to:
Silhouette Reader Service
U.S.: 3010 Walden Ave., P.O. Box 1325, Buffalo, NY 14269
Canadian: P.O. Box 609, Fort Erie, Ont. L2A 5X3

Northern Exposure
DEBRA LEE BROWN

INTIMATE MOMENTS™

Published by Silhouette Books

America's Publisher of Contemporary Romance

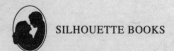 **SILHOUETTE BOOKS**

ISBN 0-373-27270-7

NORTHERN EXPOSURE

Books by Debra Lee Brown

DEBRA LEE BROWN

Award-winning author Debra Lee Brown's ongoing romance with wild and remote locales sparks frequent adventures in the Alps, the Arctic—where she has worked as a geologist—and the Sierra Nevada range of her native California. An avid outdoorswoman, Debra loves nothing better than to strand her heroes and heroines in rugged, often dangerous settings, then let nature take its course. Debra invites readers to visit her Web site at www.debraleebrown.com or to write to her c/o Harlequin Reader Service, P.O. Box 1325, Buffalo, NY 14269.

Chapter 1

A flash of camouflage through a stand of spruce, gunmetal reflecting afternoon sun. That's what had caught his attention, and was the reason he now found himself out of breath, scrambling up a hundred-yard stretch of loose volcanic scree toward a ridge topping eleven thousand feet.

This was not how he'd planned to spend his Sunday.

He sized a muddy boot print and considered that tracking a man was a hell of a lot easier than tracking an animal, especially over rugged terrain. Dead easy when the target was as green as this one obviously was.

A bald eagle circled overhead, checking him out. There were nests in the area, but those didn't concern him, not today. He paused and watched as the majestic bird dipped out of sight below the jagged tree line flanking the scree field.

The storm that had been building all morning had come to a head. Dark clouds slammed together in the sky above him. A whiff of ozone cut still air. Not unusual for late August. He resumed his climb, picking up the pace. When he topped the ridge and the sky opened, letting loose a torrent of rain, his effort was rewarded.

Twenty yards below him his prey crouched on a slab of basalt jutting into space over a thousand-foot drop-off. The man was as small as the muddy boot print had indicated. Dressed in khaki, a baseball cap pulled backward over his head, he looked *wrong*, somehow. Certainly not what he'd expected.

Then again, it was hard to tell much about him from this distance. Freeing the forty-five holstered at his hip, he picked his way carefully down the loose rubble.

Wind shrieked up from the canyon below, eddying wildly, forcing rain into horizontal sheets that changed direction without warning and threatened to knock him off balance. He was drenched in seconds.

His target fared no better. The man used his hands for balance as he edged farther out onto the precipice. As the distance between them was swallowed up, the man's intention became clear, and his own suspicions were confirmed.

A black case, the kind used to house a high-powered rifle, held his attention as he negotiated the last few feet and stepped silently onto the wet volcanic slab where the man now crouched dangerously close to the edge.

It wasn't a straight shot to the bottom of the canyon, he remembered. Jagged rocks protruded from the cliff face all the way down, providing a natural staircase for animals. But no man, to his knowledge, had ever attempted the climb.

The rock was slippery, and the rain an icy torrent that pummeled him from every direction as he edged out behind the intruder. They were both soaked to the skin. He paused, a stride away, to swipe a hank of wet hair from his eyes.

Something wasn't right.

Khaki, he thought, tightening his gaze on the man's narrow shoulders. Khaki from head to toe. The target he'd been tracking for the past two hours had worn camouflage. He was sure of it. Predator gray, flecked with green and brown, perfect for their surroundings.

Lightning flashed as a bone-white hand shot toward the black case.

"Hold it right there!" He leveled his weapon. The man whipped his head around, and he found himself staring into clear blue eyes gone wide with shock.

A *woman's* eyes.

Thunder cracked behind them in a detonation so powerful it threw him off balance. He pitched forward, scrambling for purchase. The woman jumped back, realized her mistake, then grabbed his shirt to keep from slipping over the edge.

It was no good. She screamed as she went over. He hit the rock hard, prone. Just in time, he dropped the gun and caught her wrist.

This kind of thing wasn't in his job description.

Out of the corner of his eye he caught another movement, one he'd expected. Below them, on another basaltic slab, a rare woodland caribou leaped clear of the impending danger their presence forewarned.

The woman's cap blew off, jerking his attention back to their predicament. A tumble of blond hair whipped violently in the wind, framing her heart-shaped face. She gazed up at him in mute terror. He watched as her whole life flashed before her eyes.

A heartbeat later he pulled her up and rolled with her to safety. She was on top of him; they were both drenched. Lightning shattered the sky around them, rain beat down in sheets. She'd nearly killed them both, but all that registered was how warm she felt. Warm and soft.

"Wh-who are you?" Her voice was thin and shaky, her face inches from his. He stared at her, silent, as water dripped from her trembling lips onto his mouth.

After a quick fantasy about her with him in a dry place that was anywhere but here, he came to his senses. "Game warden," he clipped. He rolled her over, pinning her under his weight. "You're under arrest."

The terror in her eyes vanished. Confusion replaced it, then rage. "Get off me!"

"No."

She fought him, but knew it was useless. He outweighed her by a good eighty pounds. Straddling her, he gripped both her wrists in one hand, pinioning them over her head, then retrieved his gun.

"Wh-what are you doing?" Fear returned to her eyes. "Let me go!"

"Woodland caribou are protected. Poachers are prosecuted."

Rain beat at them. Another clap of thunder rent the air. The storm was a good one. He liked storms.

They made everything clean again, absolved nature of her sins. Too bad it wasn't that easy with people.

She blinked through a hank of dripping hair that obscured part of her face as his words sank in. "Poachers? You mean you think I'm a *hunter?*"

"Don't play me, lady, I'm not in the mood."

"Where is he?" She tried to get up, but he wouldn't let her. For a moment he thought she meant the man he'd seen earlier through the trees. Then she twisted around, her gaze sliding to the narrow protrusion of rock where the caribou had stood.

"That bull's long gone."

She swore. It surprised him. She didn't look like the swearing type. "It's your fault. If you hadn't—hey, wait a minute!"

Ignoring her protests, he dragged her, one-handed, away from the edge, propped her against a boulder, then motioned with his gun toward the black case. "I suppose you're going to tell me that's not a rifle."

She looked at him as if he were crazy. "That's what this is about?" She nodded at the case. "You think I'm a hunter and that's a rifle."

"A poacher," he corrected.

She sucked an angry breath, and he was suddenly aware of her small breasts pushing against the wet fabric of her shirt. She caught him looking, and abruptly crossed her arms over her chest.

"Open it." She nodded at the case.

"I intend to." His weapon still trained on her, he knelt in front of the case and flipped the latches. What he saw inside didn't register.

"That's right," she said. "It's a tripod."

A *tripod?*

He swiveled toward her and gave her a good once-over. Her clothes were new. Even wet, the khaki pants still had creases pressed into them. Her boots were new, too, but not the knapsack he noticed wedged under an overhang next to where she sat glaring up at him.

"I'm a photographer."

"The hell you are." He didn't like being wrong. He was never wrong, not about something like this. Instinct told him she was lying. "Hand it over." He motioned with the gun toward her knapsack.

Another crack of thunder made them both jump. She stared at his forty-five. "Please put that away. I'm not a criminal. And shouldn't we get off this rock? We're awfully exposed up here."

She was right about that. Lightning flashed, closer this time. He fumbled, one-handed, with the knapsack, got it open and checked the contents. Film, leather canisters of varying lengths, and a heavy, professional-looking camera.

"It's a Nikon F4 with a motor drive, in case you're interested. The canisters have lenses in them. I told you, I'm a photographer, a wildlife photographer, on assignment for my magazine."

Her fingernails were polished in soft pearlescent pink, her eyebrows neatly plucked. She didn't even have a tan.

"What magazine?"

In a cool gesture that screamed arrogance, she tipped her chin at him. *"Wilderness Unlimited."*

He knew it, and most of the photographers on staff. She definitely wasn't one of them. "Let's see some ID."

He watched rainwater catch in the hollow at the base of her throat as she swallowed, flustered by his demand. "I...left it back in my rental car. On that little road off the highway."

"Yeah, right."

The west road was six miles away, over rough terrain. He couldn't believe she'd made it as far as she had on her own. Maybe she was working in concert with the guy in the camo. He did a quick three-sixty, his gaze darting over the rocky landscape toward the tree line. Nothing.

"What are you doing here?"

"I would have thought that was obvious." She blinked against the rain in the direction of the caribou's escape.

"This is a wildlife reserve. Woodland caribou is a rare species in this part of the state."

"That's exactly why I'm here."

She seemed way too sure of herself for a woman who, not five minutes ago, tumbled over the edge of a thousand-foot drop-off.

"Get up." He slid his weapon into its holster, snapped the leather trigger guard, and hoisted her knapsack off the rock.

She got to her feet, and for a long moment they just stood there, sizing each other up. She looked even smaller standing. Five-two, five-three tops. Her blond hair was plastered to her head, her clothes soaked through. The temperature was dropping fast, and he realized she was shivering.

"Come on. Let's go."

"Where?"

He relatched the tripod case and picked it up, pointing it in the direction from which he'd come. "That way. South."

"But my car's back there." She pointed west

along the barren ridge that ran for a mile or so, then dropped off into a long valley flanking the road, peppered with thick stands of timber and open meadow.

She was out here in a rainstorm with no jacket, no survival gear and no food. And a story he didn't believe. No way was he letting her out of his sight until he found out whether or not she was connected to the poacher he was sure he'd seen.

It was his job to protect the animals in the reserve against unusual disturbances. That included hunters, harebrained tourists, camo-clad mystery men and small, wet women with attitude.

"This rain could turn to snow. You'll never make it back before dark." He glanced at the roiling sky. "My station's closer. Come on."

She blocked his path, shot him a hard look that seemed comical, given her bedraggled state, and matter-of-factly relieved him of her tripod case and knapsack.

"Thanks, but I'll be fine. Besides, it's summer. This is Alaska. It doesn't really get dark until nine or ten." She turned and started back up the ridge, doing a better job of negotiating the loose volcanic scree than he expected.

Stubborn, he thought. And damned attractive. He'd been out here a long time, a year. The only other women he saw on a regular basis were Department of Fish and Game co-workers, and he only saw them a few times a month.

He ought to just let her go. Maybe he *had* made a mistake. Maybe she was who she said she was. Still, something about her was off. He watched her as she climbed steadily up the dark blanket of broken rock, and had the strangest feeling he'd seen her before.

He shook off the feeling, and scanned the tree line again for movement. Out there somewhere was another intruder, dressed head to toe in camouflage and toting more than a tripod case. Until he found out who *he* was, he wasn't letting Ms. Wilderness Unlimited out of his sight.

He let her get to the top of the ridge before he moved up behind her and looped a finger under her leather belt. It, too, looked new. He tugged.

"This way," he said, and motioned for her to follow.

"I told you, my car's *that* way."

He watched her as she slipped her arms through the straps of the knapsack, then redoubled her grip on the case. Rain ran in rivulets down her face. Her soaking clothes clung to her like a second skin. She was trim, athletic, fitter than he'd judged her to be from that first impression—the soft feel of her against him when she lay on top of him on the rock.

He moved his hand to the holster of his department-issue weapon. "Don't make me take this out again."

She shot him an incredulous look. "You can't force me to go with you."

"Wanna bet?" Two strides later he was chin to forehead with her, his hand closing firmly over her slim upper arm.

She looked him up and down, openmouthed, not the least bit afraid of him, appraising his wet uniform, her gaze flicking from his gold-tone Department of Fish and Game badge to his eyes. "What are you, some kind of wannabe cop?"

Now *that* pissed him off. "Lady, out here I *am* a cop. The only cop."

She glared up at him. "It's Wendy."

"Yeah, and I'm Peter Pan." He plucked the tripod case out of her hand and pushed her toward a little-used game trail. "Move it."

What a jerk.

The longer they walked, the angrier she got. Wendy stopped for a moment to readjust her knapsack, which had been digging into her shoulders for the past two hours. Her feet were killing her—blisters from the new boots—and her wet clothes chafed against her skin. At least the rain had stopped.

"Keep going." Warden Rambo poked her in the back. "It's not much farther."

"Good." Not breaking her stride, she shot him a nasty look over her shoulder. When she turned her attention back to the trail, she was immediately *thwacked* by a faceful of wet spruce.

Behind her, she heard him stifle a laugh.

"It's not funny." She kept moving, and every step of the way could feel his eyes on her.

They were green, flecked with gold, projecting a confidence and strength that was burned forever into her mind the first time she'd looked into them—as she dangled in space over a glacier-cut canyon, her life in his hands.

Or hand, she remembered with a shudder.

A clearing opened up ahead of them, and she stopped to catch her breath.

"Another hundred yards and we'll be there," he said as he came up behind her.

She turned to face him, and was startled for a moment by his rugged good looks. He'd been walking behind her all this time, barking out directions.

She studied him now, as a photographer studied a subject, striving for analytical clarity, for truth. What she got instead was a fluid, visceral impression that was all man.

He was tall and built. Even in wet clothes she could tell he had a great body. She should know. She'd seen enough naked hunks to last her a lifetime. His forearms were big and tanned. The muscles of his thighs were outlined in the olive drab uniform pants that, wet, fitted him like a glove.

His hands were rough from work. She knew because he'd taken one of her hands in his twice in the past hour. Once to help her over a downed spruce blocking their path, and another time because she'd gone off in the wrong direction, which wasn't hard to do out here.

As she appraised him, he cocked his head, eyeing her with more of the same suspicion he was determined not to let go of. A hank of wet, tawny hair spilled into his eyes, and she had to physically stop herself from her first reaction, which was to reach up and brush it away.

He read her intent.

She saw it in his eyes and felt suddenly uncomfortable. He was uncomfortable, too. She could tell by the way he stepped around her and pretended to look for something in the trees.

It wasn't the first time he'd done that. He'd stopped about an hour ago and had motioned for her to be quiet. He'd stood there, listening hard, eyes narrowed, darting at every shadow, as if he expected someone to pop out of the bushes and surprise them.

On impulse she said, "Thank you."

He turned to her and frowned. "For what?"

"Saving my life."

"If I hadn't stumbled, you wouldn't have gotten spooked and slipped."

"If you hadn't pointed that gun in my face," she corrected, "maybe the whole thing wouldn't have happened."

His eyes turned cold. "Come on. The station's over there."

Anger rippled up inside her, but she worked to keep it in check. That wasn't going to help her now. Besides, most of her irritation stemmed from the fact that Warden Rambo was exactly like Blake—domineering, pushy, directive.

In short, overbearing. She could think of a hundred synonyms to describe that kind of behavior. All of them got her fur up, as her dad would say.

As she followed him across the clearing, she made a minor correction to her initial judgment. He and Blake had one distinct difference. Blake's bad qualities were hidden, wrapped up in a package that was all charm. Blake was a manipulator, a snake. This guy was up front about who he was.

Which reminded her of something she'd meant to ask him. "What's your name?"

He held a broken branch aside, ushering her through a thicket choked with gooseberries, then pointed to the white lettering engraved on the black plastic name tag hanging limply from his wet shirt. "Peterson."

His arched brow told her he thought she was an idiot if she'd spent the past two hours within ten feet of him, and hadn't noticed it. She had.

"So, what should I call you? Mr. Peterson? *Warden* Peterson? Just plain old Peterson?"

"Joe," he said. "Or whatever." He moved quickly through the small stand of trees, and she followed, thinking it was a nice, simple name. Joe Peterson, game warden.

"Here it is."

She stopped in front of what he'd described to her as a station. It was really just a big cabin, one that looked as if it was built a long time ago. Constructed of rough-hewn logs, it was painted over a dull brown, like so many Forest Service or National Park buildings were these days. A big deck ran all the way around it. There was a drop-off on the far side where the deck hung out over the forest, reminding her of a tree house she'd once had when she was a girl.

Joe fished a set of keys out of his pocket, opened the door and waved her inside. The front room had a huge picture window looking out over the deck. A snowcapped mountain range loomed in the distance. A set of French doors led outside. The room was half office, half living quarters, and the contrast between the two halves was almost weird.

A computer, a multiline phone, a fax machine, and what looked to her like a shortwave radio all sat perfectly aligned on a clean desktop. Files were piled in neatly spaced stacks, sharpened pencils stood in a clean glass jar, points up, like a bouquet of flawlessly arranged flowers.

In contrast, the other side of the room looked like somebody's grandfather's mountain cabin. She liked it. Big comfortable furniture sat crowded together in front of a stone fireplace that looked as if it was used every day.

Stuffed fish and a pair of deer antlers hung on the walls. A pair of snowshoes stood in a corner jammed with skis, a rifle and a couple of pairs of well-used boots. Joe's, she thought, gauging their size.

Magazines were scattered in disarray across a coffee table that held the remains of what she guessed was his lunch: a half-eaten sandwich and a big glass of milk. Wendy's stomach growled.

"I'll get this cleaned up." He snatched the plates from the table and disappeared into another room.

While he was gone, she moved to the fireplace and studied the single, eight-by-ten photo housed in a silver filigree frame that sat alone on the varnished wooden mantel.

It was of a young woman. A blond, like her. Only not like her at all. Tall and willowy with long straight hair, the woman in the photo wore a short black cocktail dress and the most fragile, deadly innocent smile Wendy had ever seen.

She'd noticed Joe didn't wear a wedding ring, but that didn't mean anything these days.

Wendy picked up the photo as he breezed back into the room. "She's beautiful. Is she your wife?"

"Put that down."

She felt as if she were ten years old again, caught with her hand in the cookie jar. The heat of a blush warmed her cheeks. "Sorry." She quickly replaced the photo and clasped her hands together in front of her in contrition.

Wait a minute.

What was she doing? So she picked up a photograph of the guy's wife. So what? She hadn't done anything wrong. Her reaction to his censure told her she still had baggage to unload, lots of it, from her years with Blake.

"Okay, let's do this." Joe grabbed the phone off the desk and plunked down into the single office chair.

"Do what?"

"Your magazine. What's the number?"

"What?" He was going to *call* them?

"*Wilderness Unlimited.* The number."

"I heard what you said, I just don't know why you'd want to—"

"You said you were a photographer. I'm checking it out."

"Why?"

"To find out if you're telling the truth."

She couldn't believe it. "Of course I'm telling the truth. Why would I lie?"

"You tell me."

"This is ridiculous." She fisted her hands on her hips and bit back a curse.

"Fine. We'll do it the hard way." He retrieved a back issue of the nationally renowned magazine from the pile on his coffee table. A second later he was dialing the number.

"It's in New York." *You idiot.* She crossed her arms over her chest and waited. "It's what, one in the morning there?" She checked her watch, noting the four-hour time difference.

Their gazes locked. Gently, in a motion that screamed control, he placed the receiver back on the hook. She could tell he was hopping mad—not at her, but at himself for being so stupid.

The moment stretched on, until she couldn't stand the tension. "All right, fine." She walked over to the phone, dialed and handed him the receiver. "My editor's a night owl. She's probably still up."

"You know her home number by heart?"

Wendy shrugged. "She's a friend of mine." Her only friend right now.

"What's your last name?"

"Walters."

"Wendy Walters. Sounds made up."

The irony of that made her laugh.

Joe looked at her hard as he waited for someone to pick up. No one did. "She's not there," he said, and replaced the receiver.

"I guess you'll just have to trust me, then."

He struck her as a man who didn't trust anyone. He liked to be in control, have things his own way. And that was fine with her, because she was leaving.

"I'll pay you whatever you want to drive me back to my car. It can't be far from here."

"It is. You have to backtrack out of the reserve and drive around that mountain range—" he nodded at the snowcapped peaks framed in the window "—before you hit the highway again."

"I have traveler's checks and cash." She hoped he didn't want too much. All the money she had left in the world was tucked away in the small wallet in her pants.

"Doesn't matter. My truck's in the shop. Tomorrow I'll get someone to drive you. Tonight you'll stay here."

"Not a chance." She grabbed her knapsack off the couch where she'd dropped it, and tried to get by him. "I'll walk." She knew she was being ridiculous, but his bossiness irritated her.

She'd spent her whole adult life being cowed by

men who ordered her around. Well, one man. But that was over. She was done with being a "yes" girl.

He grabbed her arm as she passed. "This is your first trip to Alaska, isn't it?"

"Stop manhandling me." She pulled out of his grasp. "What if it is?"

"For starters, you have no damned idea how dangerous it is right outside that door." He nodded at where they'd come in. "Weather, bears, other predators—you wouldn't know what to do if you got into trouble."

"What makes you so sure?"

He glanced at her outfit, her boots, then swiped the knapsack out of her hand. "It's new. All of it. You're green as a stick."

Add judgmental to his list of character flaws.

She bristled but let his impression of her stand. It wasn't worth correcting. She'd be gone in the morning. She took a couple of deep breaths and resigned herself to it. "Where would I sleep?"

Their eyes met, and for a millisecond she knew the same thought that flashed across her mind also flashed across his. Now *that* was scary. At least she had an excuse. He was drop-dead gorgeous, and it had been a long time since she'd been with anyone.

On the other hand, he was exactly the kind of man she swore she'd never get involved with again. But chemistry was a funny thing. It defied logic, ignored rules.

Joe Peterson was a man who lived by rules. His own. But the room they were standing in told her that he occasionally broke them. His eyes told her, too, as he looked her over candidly in, what she knew in her gut was for him, a rare, unguarded moment.

''The sofa makes into a bed,'' he said quietly. ''There're clean towels in the bathroom. I'll get you something dry to wear.''

After they'd both showered and changed, he fixed them a hot supper of leftover chicken, tinned biscuits and homemade gravy. It was good. She was starved and ate two helpings.

Through the entire meal they didn't talk, but every once in a while she'd glance up and catch him looking at her. She'd gotten that same look a lot lately from strangers. It was as if he knew her but couldn't place her. It unnerved her and she looked away.

Later he built a fire, and they settled in front of it with steaming cups of tea. Joe paged through an Alaska Department of Fish and Game bulletin, while she stared at the photo on the mantel of the waiflike woman in the black dress.

Wendy suspected that's whose clothes she was wearing. The arms of the pink sweatshirt were too long for her, the jeans a joke. She had to roll the denim cuffs up six inches so she wouldn't trip.

She frowned, suddenly recognizing the backdrop in the photo. ''That's Rockefeller Center,'' she said without thinking. ''A professional shot, too.'' Why hadn't she noticed that before? ''What is she, a model?''

Joe looked up, and his face turned to stone.

Definitely sensitive turf. It was the second time her mention of the woman in the photo had angered him. She opted for a swift exit from the subject. ''This place is about as far from New York as you can get.''

''That's the point,'' he said, and went back to his reading.

* * *

Joe watched Wendy as she slept, curled on the sofa, a pillow tucked under her head. He wondered if her hair was as soft as it looked. The cut was short and tousled, and suited her delicate features. In the firelight it glinted gold.

From this angle she reminded him a little of Cat. Glancing at the photo on the mantel, he allowed himself a rare moment to remember her, what she was like when they were both young.

Wendy stirred, came awake in a slow, sleepy aura that was sexy as hell. Joe felt a tightening in his gut. Maybe Barb, one of his few friends in the department, was right. He needed to get out more.

"What…time is it?" Wendy propped herself up on one elbow and blinked the sleep from her eyes.

"Late. You fell asleep. I'll get you some sheets for the sofa bed."

He padded down the hall toward the back bedroom, which was used mostly for storage of department supplies. He flipped on the overhead light and went directly to the closet.

He'd never had an overnight guest at the station before. He grabbed a set of sheets, a couple of blankets, and was ready to switch the light off when he spied a stack of tabloids he'd meant to burn.

Barb brought him all kinds of reading material on her once-a-week trips to the station. He'd told her to stop buying him these trashy newspapers, but she just kept on. Might as well read something fun once in a while, she'd say.

He grabbed the stack to take them out to the fire, and did a double take.

The edition on top was dated three weeks ago. He stared at the photo on the cover. Two men and a woman. The shot barely disguised the fact that they were naked.

He remembered now. He'd read the tabloid article because he recognized the name of one of the men in the picture. Cat had known him, had talked about him. But it wasn't the man who concerned him, it was the woman.

That's why she looked so damned familiar!

Joe committed the tabloid headline to memory before carrying the blankets and sheets back down the hall. He paused in the doorway to the front room. His *guest* was looking at Cat's photo again. He glared at her back, the headline playing in his mind like a bad record—

New York Fashion Photographer Willa Walters Overexposed in Deadly Sex/Drug scandal.

Chapter 2

If he was cool to her before, he was downright icy now.

Wendy stepped barefoot onto the wet wood deck and closed the French doors behind her. Joe stood with his back to her, gazing out at a late-night sunset whose colors looked as if they'd jumped off an artist's palette. She was tempted to go back inside and get her camera.

The rain had stopped and the sky was clearing. Dark clouds still thrashed above them but eased into violet tipped with brilliant orange near the horizon. The snowcapped peaks in the distance looked like pink snow cones from a county fair. Wendy had never seen a more beautiful sky in her life.

Or a more tightly wound man.

Aware of her approach, Joe began to pace back and forth along the length of the deck, his hand skimming the railing. He reminded her of a caged predator. A very irritated caged predator. The question on her mind was *Why?*

He'd dumped the sheets and blankets on the sofa bed, mumbled a good-night, then had retreated outside to the deck, seemingly to watch the sunset. She knew that wasn't the reason he was out there. He didn't know her well enough for her to have made him so angry, but apparently she had. Or something had.

At this point she didn't care. She had her own problems. She had three weeks to get those caribou photographs to the magazine. Three short weeks.

When the senior editor at *Wilderness Unlimited,* a sorority sister from college, had agreed to Wendy's proposal, she'd been ecstatic. It was the first break she'd gotten since *the incident,* since life, as she'd known it, had blown up in her face. She knew it was the only break she was likely to get, and she was determined not to waste it.

A cleansing breath of cool air laced with wet spruce cleared her head. Supper, and the nap, had bolstered her strength. She was still a bit jet-lagged from the long flight west. That, and the fact that there were about sixteen hours of daylight at this latitude this time of year, played havoc with her internal clock.

"Warden," she said as she moved toward him across the wet deck, thinking it best to keep their communications formal.

He stopped pacing, his back to her, but didn't respond.

Unfolding a map she'd retrieved from her knapsack, she said, "There's something I want to ask you."

He didn't even acknowledge her with a look when she joined him at the railing. ''That buck today, the woodland caribou...''

''Bull,'' he said.

''Excuse me?''

''Caribou males are called bulls in Alaska, not bucks. I thought you would have known that, being a wildlife photographer.''

''I, uh...'' He had a way of flustering her with his offhand comments. She was determined not to let him back her down. ''The point is...I need to find him again.''

''Why?''

''I told you. For the magazine. My assignment.''

He turned to look at her, crossing his arms over his chest and hiking a hip onto the railing, as if settling in for a friendly chat. His eyes, however, were anything but friendly. *''Wilderness Unlimited.* So you said.''

She moved closer, spun the map around and spread it across the railing so he could see it. ''I left my car here.'' She pointed to a spot on the highway, then traced her finger along the route she'd taken into the reserve. ''I first saw the bull here, where you—''

''How much experience do you have?''

''What?'' She looked up at him.

''With wildlife photography. What other animals have you photographed?''

Besides the menagerie of pets she'd had growing up and her college's mascot, a Clydesdale, the answer was none. Well, except for some small animals she'd seen earlier today. But she wasn't about to tell *him* that. His smug expression and arched brow told her he couldn't wait to point out her shortcomings.

Blake had been like that. Always making sure she knew she wasn't good enough, wasn't experienced enough. At every opportunity, hammering it home that she was nothing without him.

Well, here's a news flash: Blake was wrong.

It had taken her a long time to see it. Weeks of getting over the shock of what had happened in New York, lying in the dark on the twin bed in her old room in her parents' house, thinking about her life—what she wanted, what she was, what she could be.

Her new life started now. And she wasn't going to let any man, particularly one who didn't even know her, tell her she wasn't capable of handling it.

"Moose," she said. The lie came easy. "Deer, wolves, humpback whales, penguins. You name it, I've photographed it."

"Really?" He perked right up, seeming to believe her. She felt good all of a sudden. Better than she had all evening. "Where'd you shoot the penguins? Antarctica?"

She supposed she shouldn't make up anything that seemed too farfetched. If you're going to lie, stick as close to the truth as possible. She'd read that once in a detective novel.

"No," she said. "Right here in Alaska. In the, uh, arctic."

"No kidding?" Joe smiled, his eyes glittering appreciatively in the last of the light. It was the first smile she'd seen from him, and a little shiver raced through her. Things were back on track.

"Anyway, about that bull..." She pushed the map toward him again.

"You must be pretty famous, then."

"Who, me? No, not at all. I'm just another photographer.'' She pointed to the spot on the map where they'd last seen the bull, but Joe Peterson wasn't looking at the map. He was looking at her.

''I'll have to disagree with you, *Wendy.''* He said her name as if it were a foreign word. ''It would take one hell of a photographer, wildlife or otherwise, to shoot pictures of penguins in Alaska.''

Why was he so antagonistic? What did he care if she had or hadn't photographed—

''Because, *Wendy*—'' there it was again ''—there aren't any penguins in Alaska.''

''There…aren't?''

''They're a southern hemisphere species. Any wildlife photographer would know that.'' He pushed away from the deck and started back inside.

She followed him. ''All right, I lied. So what? I still need to get those photos for the magazine, and to do that I'll need to find that buck or bull or whatever it is again, or another one like it.''

He marched into the kitchen and started washing their supper dishes as if she wasn't even there, banging plates around, sloshing water out of the sink.

She muscled in beside him and spread the map out on the dish drainer. ''You're right. I don't know anything about penguins, okay? But I do know that there are only a handful of woodland caribou in Alaska. They're rare, elusive, completely unlike the native species that roams the tundra. No one has ever photographed them before.''

''There's a reason for that,'' he said, and plopped the dish he was working on back in the water. ''It's dangerous. The males are rogues. They're skittish as hell and thrive in cliff settings just like the one you nearly got us both killed on.''

She couldn't think about that. "I need those pictures. It's important. I'm not asking you to help me, I'm simply asking you to show me on this map where I might find more caribou, bulls especially."

He snorted and went back to his dishwashing. She noticed how strong his hands were, how tanned they looked against the white plastic plates. For a millisecond she recalled them on her body that afternoon. In a blood-heating thought that had nothing to do with photography, she wondered what the contrast would be like of his bronze hands against her bare white skin.

"It doesn't matter," he said, and grabbed a towel. "That bull we saw today, along with any others in the area, will have bolted to the other side of the reserve. You can't drive there. You'd have to go on foot." He gave her a once-over, his eyes lingering for a second on her mouth. "A woman like you would never make it."

She knew it was Joe Peterson, game warden, standing before her, saying the words, but it was Blake Barrett's voice she heard in her head.

"Oh, really?" She stormed out of the kitchen, slapped the map on the coffee table—which, earlier, she'd moved out of the way—and proceeded to make up the sofa bed with the sheets he'd delivered.

Joe leaned in the door frame and watched her. The longer he looked at her, the angrier she got. What was it about men that they assumed—*assumed* without even knowing her—that she wasn't up to the task at hand, no matter what that task happened to be?

From something as simple as carting out the garbage to something as complex as managing a runway shoot, or as challenging as finding a couple of caribou in the mountains—guys like Blake Barrett, and now Joe Peterson, thought she was helpless.

Well, hide and watch, boys.

She snapped the crisp white sheet over the foam mattress.

Hide and watch.

Joe thrashed around in bed until the top sheet was twisted around his legs like a rope. He ripped it from his body and tossed it aside, then punched up the pillows, ramming his head into them like a Dall sheep in full rut.

It was no good.

He'd been lying there for the past hour and a half, wide awake. The bright-green numbers on the digital clock by the bed read just past two in the morning. After their conversation on the deck, which had turned into an argument in the kitchen, he'd left his overnight guest to fend for herself and had retreated to the bedroom to sleep.

Only sleep hadn't come. He'd reread the tabloid article he'd found in the back bedroom, paying particular attention to the reporter's assessment of Willa Walters—the woman who was sleeping on his sofa bed. He knew these kinds of newspapers twisted the facts to suit their story and sensationalized every tidbit. All the same, he couldn't get the sordid details out of his mind. He couldn't shrug it off and let it go.

The other thing he couldn't let go of was the idea that the two of them weren't alone out here. He'd definitely seen a man in the woods that afternoon. On the hike back to the station earlier that evening, he could have sworn that someone was following them. It could be a poacher, as he'd first suspected, or maybe a lost tourist. Hell, for all he knew it could be a tabloid reporter following the Walters story all the way to Alaska, though he didn't think it very likely.

He rolled onto his stomach into a sprawl, working to get comfortable, forcing all thoughts of mystery men and lying photographers from his mind. He willed himself to sleep. A few minutes later, relaxed at last, he was almost there, hovering on the edge.

Then he heard it, the faint creak of board outside on the deck.

A second later he was up, pulling on jeans and a shirt in the dark, scrambling for his boots, taking care to be as quiet as possible. He realized his heart was beating fast, much faster than normal, but it wasn't because he feared what was out there.

He'd run into all kinds of things in the night out here—hikers, department personnel on reconnaissance, even wildlife photographers. Most of the time it was animals: a disoriented grizzly, groggy from hibernation, ambling onto the deck, raccoons digging in his trash bin, the odd moose or mountain lion. None of them were dangerous if you respected their space.

No, the reason for his accelerated heart rate wasn't that he feared for his own safety. He did, however, fear for the safety of the woman sleeping in his front room. More accurately, he feared she'd wake up and do something stupid that would land her in trouble.

That creaking board wasn't a figment of his imagination.

Joe stepped lightly down the darkened hallway, peering into the bathroom and kitchen, and out the kitchen windows before slipping silently into the front room.

His house guest was asleep, the covers pulled over her head. Everything was quiet except for the night-time sounds of crickets and a light wind breezing through the trees. Joe moved to the window and looked out.

He stood, frozen in place, for a full minute, his gaze sweeping the deck, the steps leading up to it, and the forest beyond. A sliver of moon poked through the clouds, casting an eerie light on the trees, painting every surface ghostly gray.

Light exploded from the room's overhead fixture.

Joe whirled toward the switch.

"What's up?" Wendy leaned sleepily against the wall flanking him, squinting against the light, her hand still on the switch.

In a lightning-fast move, he flicked it off, grabbed her around the waist and backed them away from the window.

"Hey, what the—"

"Quiet!" Setting her on her feet, he looked at her hard, his eyes readjusting to the dark, and made a sign for her to be still.

"What's wrong?" she whispered.

He didn't answer. Pushing her back into the shadow of the door frame, he moved to the corner of the room by the fireplace and plucked his rifle from where it stood upright next to a jumble of snow-shoes and skis.

He knew it was loaded, but checked it anyway, then listened hard for a moment to the ordinary sounds of the night. Wendy stood stock-still in the door frame, listening, too, moonlight bathing her face in a soft pearl wash. Her hair shone silver and swished lightly against her neck as she turned toward him.

It suddenly struck him how beautiful she was, standing there in nothing more than the old T-shirt he'd loaned her to sleep in. His T-shirt. It looked entirely different on her than it did on him.

Of course it did, doofus.

The fire in the hearth had died, and the room was cold. Her nipples stood out against the fabric of the thin shirt. She pushed off suddenly, from bare foot to bare foot, as if the floor were icy. His gaze was drawn to her small feet, upward along lithe, toned legs to the hem of the T-shirt. For a long moment he thought about what was under that T-shirt.

"Is something out there?" She looked pointedly at the rifle in his hands.

"I don't know." He moved up beside her, then in front of her, and, when the moon disappeared behind a cloud, strode quickly across the room to the front door.

Wendy followed.

He turned, ready to tell her to go back, but it was too late. She was right there with him, her face lighting up in anticipation, as she waited for him to open the door. No fear. Not even a hint of it. Just wide-eyed curiosity. It genuinely surprised him. She was a New York fashion photographer for God's sake. He knew native Alaskans, women born and bred to the life here, who would have been fearful, at least cautious, in the same situation.

But not Ms. Wendy, Willa, whatever-her-name-was Walters. Caution was not a part of her makeup. That had been apparent yesterday on the cliff face.

"Are you going out there?"

"Yeah. Stay here, and lock the door after I leave."

She placed a warm hand on his arm as he turned the lock, and the shock of it sent an odd shiver through him. "Be careful," she said.

The whole idea of her saying that to him made him smile. It was a slow smile that rolled over his features. He felt it inside, too. It was the damnedest thing, her telling *him* to be careful.

Their gazes met, and for a few seconds he allowed himself to look at her. It had been a long time since he'd slept with a woman, even longer since he'd had one in his life on a regular basis. He missed it more than he'd let on to himself. He missed it a lot, he realized, his gaze slipping to her mouth, her breasts, those tiny bare feet.

He told himself he wasn't attracted to *her,* just her body, her looks. She was a woman, and he was a man in need of a good—

She removed her hand from his arm.

The sordid facts of the incident involving her in New York, described in raunchy detail in the tabloid article, crash landed in his mind. It was all too close to home, and made him remember things he'd tried for the past year to forget.

"Go back to bed," he said stiffly. Redoubling his grip on the rifle, he eased the front door open and stepped into the night.

Wendy came awake with a start, sitting bolt upright on the sofa bed's lumpy foam mattress. Bad dream, she realized, and forced herself to draw a calming breath. Nightmare, really—the same one she had over and over about her and Blake and what had happened that night in a Manhattan loft.

Swiveling out of bed, she banished the memory from her mind and wondered if Joe was still outside. The luminous dial of her watch read 3:00 a.m., about an hour from the time he'd left the cabin. She'd waited up for him awhile, curled on the sofa bed, but had fallen asleep. Walking to the window, she looked out. It would be dawn soon. The cloud cover had dissipated, revealing a cobalt blanket of sky peppered with stars.

When she turned toward the hall, pausing in the doorway, she glanced at the stack of skis and snow-shoes in the corner of the room by the fireplace and noticed Joe's rifle wasn't there. Maybe he was still outside. Maybe he'd found something.

Yesterday, from the moment she'd discovered the caribou and had started tracking it, she could have sworn she wasn't alone. Someone, not Joe, had been out there with her. She knew it wasn't Joe because he'd shown her on the map yesterday afternoon the route he'd taken from the station. He'd only inter-cepted her by chance. She'd covered territory he hadn't even been in that day, and she'd had com-pany.

The thought of it gave her the creeps.

Shaking it off, she padded down the hallway to-ward the bathroom and noticed that the door to the bedroom was open. On impulse she moved toward it.

Joe Peterson was a strange animal. He reminded her a little of the rogue bull whose photo she'd been so desperate to shoot yesterday on the rock. He lived out here alone, miles from anywhere and anyone, in a world where he was master. At least, he thought he was. That made everyone else a mere minion, a position with which Wendy was overly familiar and was determined never to assume again.

She'd spent years working with all kinds of people. Except for her bad judgment where Blake was concerned, she considered herself a pretty good judge of character. Something told her there was a good reason for Joe Peterson's less than friendly behavior toward her. By the end of the evening his cool indifference had turned to outright irritation, and it bothered her that she couldn't fathom a reason.

Intuition told her he was a man in pain. That alone should have set off a loud warning bell in her thick head. Men in pain were a problem for her. The problem was she couldn't not help them. Her natural instinct was to nurture, be a helpmate. That's what had gotten her into trouble with Blake. Over the years being a helpmate had turned into being a doormat.

Never again.

At the door of Joe's bedroom she stopped, remembering the fleeting moment before he'd gone outside, rifle in hand, recalling the way he'd looked at her mouth, her body, and had made her heartbeat quicken. There was no doubt she was attracted to him, and he to her. She hadn't bothered fighting it because in the morning someone would take her back to her car and she'd never see him again.

The thought of that wasn't as soothing as it should have been.

The bed in Joe's room was empty, pillows askew, sheets twisted into a pile on the floor. Moonlight flooded the airy space. The room smelled like him, cool and green and unstable. Those were the impressions that had taken hold of her when she'd touched his arm, when she'd stood so close to him she'd felt his breath on her face.

With a start she realized the rifle he'd taken outside with him was propped against the wall by the bed. Without thinking, she took a step into the room, then swallowed a gasp.

Joe sat in a big Adirondack chair by a row of old-fashioned windows overlooking the deck. Clad only in jeans, his chest was bare, the muscles in his arms tight. There were no drapes on the windows. His face, reflecting some terrible pain, was bathed in the bright light of an August moon.

Her gaze followed his to the framed photo he'd moved to the antique nightstand. Wendy hadn't even noticed it was missing from the mantel.

All at once she knew.

"She's dead, isn't she?"

Slowly, as if he'd known all along she was standing there, Joe turned to look at her. "Yes."

"I'm so sorry."

"Why?"

She felt awkward all of a sudden, her tongue thick in her mouth. "I…"

"Go back to sleep, Ms. Walters."

"I wish you'd call me Wendy."

He rose from the chair and placed the photo face-down into a drawer. "How about Willa?"

Chapter 3

It was hard to pretend she hadn't gotten under his skin, but he forced himself.

Joe poured Willa Walters a cup of black coffee, and while she sat at the kitchen table and drank it, he fixed them a quick breakfast.

"It's not my real name," she said after the silence between them stretched to a breaking point.

"Wendy?"

"No, Willa." She shot him an irritated look. "It was made up for me."

"By who?"

She shrugged. "A man I used to know."

"One of the guys in that picture?"

The shock that registered on her face turned instantly to annoyance. "I didn't know game wardens read those kinds of newspapers."

He flashed her a look, but didn't respond. He divided a panful of scrambled eggs between two plates, topped them with buttered toast and handed her one.

He expected her to refuse it, but she didn't. Silently she accepted the food and began to eat. That was another thing that surprised him about her—she had one hell of an appetite for someone so petite.

"That picture isn't what you think." She glanced up at him as he joined her at the table. "We weren't... you know."

"Buck naked?"

She speared him with a nasty smirk. "The male models were wearing Speedos. I was in a strapless tank suit. The tabloid cropped the photo to make the situation seem like something it wasn't. The whole thing was completely innocent. I was on a shoot—at a public beach, for God's sake. Besides, that photo had nothing to do with the incident."

He let that bit of information sink in while he watched her viciously jab a forkful of scrambled egg.

This morning she had dressed in her own clothes again, and had left Cat's sweatshirt and jeans in a neatly folded pile on the made-up sofa bed. Her feet were bare, except for the squares of moleskin she'd applied to her blisters. She sat sideways on her chair, her legs crossed, affording him a good view of her slender ankles. Her toenails were polished, too, he noticed.

"New boots?" He nodded at her bandaged feet.

"New everything. My luggage was stolen at the airport, so I had to buy all new stuff."

"Fairbanks or Anchorage?" That kind of thing didn't happen too often in Alaska.

"Anchorage, when I first arrived. A guy nabbed my suitcase off the conveyor and took off with it.

Thank God I had my camera bag on me. I'd never be able to afford to replace my Nikon.''

He watched her as she finished her toast. A dab of butter clung to the edge of her lip, and he caught himself wondering what it would feel like, what she would taste like, if he flicked it away with his tongue.

His attraction to her disgusted him.

He adjusted his position on the hard kitchen chair and croaked, ''Tough break,'' not really meaning it. Someone like her deserved what she got.

''Yeah, well...'' She waved her fork in the air in a dismissive gesture. ''That's the least of my worries at this point.''

''I'll bet.''

She shot him a cool look and continued eating.

With his back to her, as he rinsed out the coffee carafe and ground beans for another pot, he asked her about some of the things he'd read about her in the tabloid article. She immediately changed the subject.

''The only other road into the reserve is this one.'' She whipped the folded map—the one she'd tried to get him to look at last night—out of her pants pocket and spread it on the table. ''If I leave my car here—'' she pointed to a remote spot on a little-used Jeep trail ''—and walk in from the east...''

''You're likely to get yourself killed.''

She glared up at him.

''Besides, the caribou won't be there. They'll be here.'' He leaned over the table and jabbed a finger at another spot, more than forty miles from where she was planning on leaving her car.

''Oh.'' Her expression darkened as she considered

exactly what a forty-mile hike in a remote Alaskan wilderness area meant.

He felt the beginnings of a smile edge his lips. It vanished as she cleared her throat, sat up tall in her chair—those ridiculously perky breasts of hers jutting forward—and in a bright voice said, "Fine."

He snorted. "You're a piece of work."

And that was the straw that finally broke the camel's back. Her blue eyes glittered with anger. She pressed her lips tightly together and waited, as if counting to ten, then she let him have it.

"What is it with you? You've been rude to me from the moment we met. You read a bunch of twisted half-truths in some supermarket tabloid and you think you know everything about me. Which you don't," she emphasized.

"Even if all of it were true—which it isn't—what do you care? What business is it of yours? That badge—" she flashed her eyes at the Department of Fish and Game emblem on his shirt "—doesn't give you license to be a jerk."

He enjoyed watching her while she ranted at him. Her cheeks blazed with color, her eyes turned the warmest shade of blue he'd ever seen. Abruptly she stood and came around the table at him. He didn't know whether he wanted to toss her out the door onto her very shapely ass or back her up against the refrigerator and lay one on her.

A snappy retort died on his lips as the sound of an approaching vehicle interrupted their conversation.

"What's that?" she said, turning toward the window.

"Your ride outta here."

''About time.''

She followed him into the front room as the sounds of a car door slamming and footfalls scrunching across gravel drew their attention to the front door.

It opened, and Barb Maguire, dressed in a neatly pressed department-issue uniform, breezed into the room. ''Hi-ya, Joe!'' She saw Wendy and did a double take. ''Oh.'' Her gaze washed over first Wendy, then him. When she recovered from her obvious shock, a smile bloomed on her face. ''Hi, I'm Barb, Joe's delivery girl, so to speak.''

She handed him a stack of mail and what looked like a month's worth of department paperwork. ''Thanks,'' he said.

The two women shook hands. Wendy introduced herself and made some polite small talk as Barb assessed the situation: Cat's clothes on the sofa bed next to the pile of neatly folded blankets and bed sheets, two empty tea cups on the coffee table and a heap of dead ashes in the hearth.

She flashed him a conspiratorial look, grinning like the cat who ate the canary, when Wendy turned to grab her knapsack off a chair. He put on his best it's-not-what-you-think expression, but it didn't deter her.

Barb Maguire, a DF&G technician who was married to the department's local wildlife biologist, had been trying to play matchmaker for him for the past year. Her goal was to get him into town so she could fix him up with one of her girlfriends. Joe wasn't interested, but Barb was relentless.

''So, you're a wildlife photographer. That's...well, perfect!'' She winked at Joe.

"Uh, yeah. I'm here to photograph woodland caribou."

"Whoa. Tough assignment." Barb nodded in admiration.

Joe had had enough. "I told her she'd be a damned fool to go looking for them on her own."

"Do you think everyone is a helpless idiot, or is it just me?"

He started to answer, but Barb cut him off. "No, he thinks that about pretty much everybody." She grinned. "Don't let it put you off."

"I don't intend to." With a dismissive swing of her hair, Wendy did an about-face and retrieved her socks and boots from where they'd dried overnight by the hearth. She struggled to get them on comfortably over the moleskin.

Joe resisted an overpowering urge to help her.

"Why not hire a guide?" Barb said.

"Can't afford it." Wendy laced the stiff boots, grimacing. "I'm covering my expenses myself. Besides, I don't want a guide."

"Why don't *you* take her?" Barb arched a thick, dark brow at him. "You know every inch of the reserve and exactly where those caribou are likely to hole up."

"No!" he and Wendy said in unison.

"Whoa. Sorry. I thought you two were...uh, friends."

"We're not," Joe said.

"My mistake."

Wendy's cheeks flushed scarlet. "I'll, um, be right back." She headed down the hall toward the bathroom, and when they heard the door close, Barb was all over him.

"Who is she? She's great! Where did you meet her? What happened with the two of you last—"

"I want you to take her back to her rental car out on the west road, then follow her to the highway. I want her out of here. Got it?"

Barb's brown eyes widened. "Got it."

"And don't ask," he said, as she opened her mouth to fire more questions at him.

A moment later Wendy's footsteps cut short their conversation. "Okay, I'm ready." She turned to him and stiffly offered her hand. Feeling awkward, he shook it. "Thank you for your…hospitality." Her tone pushed the sarcastic-meter off the scale.

At the door their gazes met and, for the briefest moment, in her eyes he read the same unguarded fusion of emotions he'd seen in them last night when she was standing in his bedroom: compassion, longing, regret.

He was familiar with the last one. God, was he ever.

Barb called to him over the roof of her department pickup before she climbed inside. "Almost forgot. Your truck's out of the shop. Couple of guys from the garage are bringing it up later this morning."

"Thanks," he said, then stood in the open doorway and watched as Barb turned her pickup around and drove Wendy Walters out of his life.

Good riddance.

But fifteen minutes later, he couldn't stop himself from making the call.

"Wilderness Unlimited," the operator uttered in an East Coast accent.

When Joe reached the senior editor, Wendy's story was confirmed.

She was out here to shoot the caribou, only it wasn't the magazine's idea. It was Wendy's. A photo essay slated for next month's edition had fallen through, and Wendy had cut a deal with the editorial director to hire her as a staff photographer if she could deliver the caribou photos before the issue went to press. No small feat.

"No one's ever photographed them up close," Joe said into the receiver.

"That's exactly why our little Wendy picked that particular project. She knew the magazine's director would be champing at the bit for a coup like that. He couldn't resist."

"She must want that job pretty bad."

"She's desperate," the woman said. "Can't say I blame her. After what happened in that loft with that model—geez, he was only twenty-nine, Wendy's age. So sad. They say it was an overdose of ecstasy or crack, I don't remember which. Anyway—"

"I get the picture," Joe said, not wanting to rehash the details he'd read in the tabloid.

"She's trying to start over, make a new life for herself. Getting away from Blake Barrett is the smartest thing she's ever done. She should have done it years ago. That snake didn't even have the decency to speak to the police on her behalf."

Blake Barrett. Joe wondered who he was. Ex-husband, maybe? Lover? Her boss?

"You take care of our girl, now. I worry about her out there on her own."

Joe didn't bother telling her that the photographer formerly known as Willa Walters was on her way back to the highway as they spoke. Next month's issue would have to run without those caribou photos, and the petite blond who'd initiated a wild night of kinky sex and drugs resulting in the death of a male fashion model would have to find herself another assignment.

Preferably as far away from him as possible.

"You don't say?" Barb slowed the green Department of Fish and Game pickup into the turnoff from the highway onto the spur road where Wendy had left her rental car.

"Yeah. The issue goes to press in three weeks. I've got to get those photos."

She rummaged around in her knapsack, searching for her sunglasses. She pulled them out, along with an envelope crafted of high-quality stationery on which she'd scribbled some phone numbers. She'd been carrying the envelope around in her camera bag for the past ten days, ever since it had shown up in her parents' mailbox.

The letter inside had been from Blake. When Wendy realized it, she'd kept the envelope with the phone numbers, and tossed the letter, unread, into her parents' recycling bin—which was exactly where it belonged.

"Joe's not gonna like it," Barb said, jolting her back to the present. "You going in there on your own."

Wendy stuffed the envelope back in her bag, and made a huffy sound. "It's none of his business."

"Don't try telling him that. Joe Peterson thinks everything that goes on within a hundred miles of him is his business, and he wants it run his way."

"Tell me about it." Wendy smiled at her, and they both laughed.

Barb Maguire, a sturdily built woman in her early thirties with springy black ringlets framing a cherublike face, was a breath of fresh air after spending the past fifteen hours with Warden Bug-up-His-Butt. Although, Wendy had to admit, it *was* a pretty nice butt.

"Seriously, if you're planning on hiking into the east side of the reserve, you'd best be prepared for bears and bad weather."

"I'm no amateur, despite appearances." And despite the fact that it had been years since she'd done any camping or hiking. But she didn't mention that fact to Barb. "I've got a carload of backpacking gear I know how to use and some emergency flares in case I get into trouble."

Barb glanced speculatively at her half-empty knapsack.

"This is just my camera bag. I had no idea I was going to be out for more than a quick stretch of the legs yesterday. I spotted that caribou, and when he took off, I had to follow. There wasn't time to go back to the car to get my gear."

"Yeah," Barb said, "those rogue bulls are just like men, aren't they? Let 'em out of your sight for a minute and they're history."

Wendy laughed. "Speaking of history…and rogue bulls…" She looked pointedly at Barb.

"Ahh, so I was right about you two. Good. It's about time he started living again."

Wendy shook her head. "No, you were wrong, but I'm still curious. What's his story?"

"Joe?" Barb sucked in a breath and readjusted her hands on the steering wheel. Shaking her head, she said, "He just can't seem to get over it. Cat's death, I mean."

So that was her name. Cat Peterson. It fit her. "She was a beautiful woman."

"You saw the picture."

Wendy nodded.

"She was just a kid, really. Twenty-two. Nine years younger than Joe when she died."

Wendy wanted to know more, but didn't want to seem as interested as she obviously was. The question was *why* was she so interested? Men like Joe Peterson were bad news. The last thing she needed was another warden in her life. Blake had given an award-winning performance in that role for the past seven years.

"Joe lived for Cat," Barb said. "When she died, he just retreated. Took that job up in the reserve, closed himself off from everyone and everything."

"I didn't know the Department of Fish and Game made remote assignments like that." Before she'd left New York, she'd done some checking on the game reserve's management.

"They don't. But when that herd of woodland caribou were discovered out here last year, Fish and Wildlife Protection wanted somebody in the reserve for at least a season. Couldn't get any takers."

"So Joe volunteered."

"You got it. First time the two agencies ever collaborated like this. Fish and Wildlife is technically part of the Alaska State Troopers."

Wendy remembered Joe's handgun. "Well, he certainly seems to be into the role, if you know what I mean. He really is a control freak, isn't he?"

"Big-time. Which is probably the reason he

blames himself for Cat's death. Though I don't know
what he could have done to have stopped it. Cat was
a grown woman. He couldn't keep her under lock
and key, now, could he? No matter how much he
wanted to protect her.''

Joe *was* the protective type. Wendy knew that for
a fact from yesterday's little adventure. She could
have made it back to her car last night before dark.
She would have been dog tired, but she could have
done it. All the same, no way a guy like Joe Peterson
would have let her hike all that way on her own.

"How did Cat die?" she asked.

"Drug overdose. In New York last year. She was
a fashion model, just starting out. Got mixed up with
the wrong crowd, I guess."

"Oh, God." Wendy felt as if someone had
punched her.

In her mind she sifted through the faces of the
young female models she'd met at parties and industry events. Her own work with Blake had been
mostly for men's magazines like *Esquire* and *GQ*.
She generally didn't work with women. She knew
she'd never met Cat, but wondered if Blake had.

"I, uh, recognize you from your pictures," Barb
said.

Wendy's stomach continued to roll. Even out here
in the middle of nowhere, she couldn't get away from
her past.

Barb shot a glance at the supermarket tabloid
sticking out from under a fast-food bag on the dash
of the pickup. "They're still following the story."

No wonder Joe Peterson had looked at her as if
she were the lowest form of life on earth. Sometimes
that's exactly what she felt like. She wasn't proud of

some of the things she'd allowed herself to be sucked into, but that was over now.

And no wonder he was so angry—at her and himself. Wendy knew Joe was physically attracted to her, and had been from the moment he'd pulled her up onto the rock and saved her life. Once he'd realized who she was—sometime after supper and before bed, she guessed—that attraction would have been hard to reconcile, especially for a man like Joe. Given the way Cat had died, and given what he'd read about Wendy in the papers...

"Pull over," Wendy said, reaching for the door handle. She thought she might be sick.

"Just about to. That's your rental, isn't it? A blue Explorer?"

She nodded, working to keep her breakfast down.

Stepping out of the truck, Wendy took a few deep breaths and felt better. Fishing the SUV's keys out of her pocket, she frowned at the driver's side door. It was unlocked. She was sure she'd locked it.

"Everything okay?" Barb called from her pickup.

"Um, yeah. Fine." But it wasn't fine. She was *sure* she'd locked it. "Barb, about those tabloids..."

"Oh, heck, don't worry about it. No way I believe all the stuff they wrote about you."

She tossed her knapsack in the Explorer, then smiled. "Thanks."

"All set, then?"

One last question burned inside her. She had to ask it.

"How long were they married? Joe and Cat," she added, when Barb's thick brows wrinkled in confusion.

"Cat wasn't Joe's wife," Barb said. "She was his kid sister."

* * *

Joe snatched the phone on the fourth ring. ''Peterson.'' He'd been outside fixing a broken water pipe that ran from the spring up the hill into the cabin.

''Hey, it's me.'' Barb's normally cheerful voice had an edge to it he didn't like.

''What's up?''

''Wendy Walters. I just thought you'd want to know.''

Joe pulled the phone onto his lap and slung a hip on the edge of the desk. ''Know what?''

''She's planning on hiking in over the east ridge after those caribou. That gun-sight pass—you know the one.''

''Son of a bitch!''

''I know, I know. Don't kill the messenger. The whole first hour in the pickup I tried to talk her out of it, but she's dead set on it.''

''How long ago'd you drop her?''

'''Bout two hours ago. My radio's on the blink. Had to wait till I got back to headquarters to call you.''

There wasn't any cell coverage in the area. Hell, the closest town was 150 miles away.

''All right, all right. I gotta go.'' He started to put the handset down.

''Goin' after her?''

He put the receiver back to his ear. ''What do you think?''

The last thing Joe heard before he slammed the phone down on the desk was Barb Maguire's trademark titter.

Chapter 4

It took him six hours to catch up to her.

And when he did, Joe realized his temper had ratcheted to dangerous proportions. ''Get a grip, Peterson,'' he cautioned himself. He was determined to handle this like a professional.

By the time he was able to gather his gear, get his truck out of the shop and break just about every traffic law on the books racing to the eastern edge of the reserve, Wendy Walters had gained a huge head start on him.

Still, he would have bet his next paycheck that he would have overtaken her miles ago, that she would never have made it as far as the steep, glacier-cut canyon he was now traversing. He would have lost that bet, he realized, as he caught a flash of movement on the sheer rock face a quarter of a mile ahead of him.

Instinctively he reached for the pair of Austrian-made binoculars secured to his chest by a well-worn leather harness. "I'll be a son of a—" He bit off the curse as he peered through the field glasses.

Wendy Walters, wannabe wildlife photographer, trudged up the steep, rocky trail toward the narrow gun-sight pass marking the little-used eastern entrance to the reserve. Joe checked his watch. 7:00 p.m. She'd made damned good time. The woman was fit, he'd give her that.

But he was fitter, and right now he was fit to be tied.

He secured the binoculars, hunched his department-issue backpack high on his hips, recinching the padded belt, and took off at a jog. The weather looked iffy. Another storm was moving in from the west, coming right at them. Dark clouds massed overhead, obscuring a late-summer sun that had already dipped well below the jagged, snowcapped peaks surrounding the canyon.

Now that he'd found her, he didn't intend to let her out of his sight, even for a second. He'd parked his truck next to her rented SUV at the end of the gravel road, miles behind them, and had spotted her small boot prints the moment he'd started up the muddy trail toward the reserve.

What bothered him was that two miles back he'd picked up another set of boot prints, twice as large as Wendy's and leaving deep impressions in the soft earth. They definitely weren't alone out here.

There hadn't been another vehicle parked near Wendy's Explorer, or anywhere along the gravel road, but that didn't mean anything. There were dozens of spur roads, and twenty different ways to intersect the trail they were on, if one was prepared to hike cross-country.

Remembering yesterday's glimpse of Camo Man, Joe scanned the shadowed crevices of the canyon, then picked up the pace, fixing his gaze on the petite woman ahead of him, trudging steadily upward toward the pass, dwarfed by the bright-blue pack on her back.

"What are *you* doing here?" Wendy said, when he finally caught up with her.

"That's my line." He grabbed her arm and jerked her toward him.

"Hey!"

He eyed her up and down, inspecting her for signs of injury or fatigue. He saw neither. In fact, he noticed she'd barely broken a sweat, which was nothing short of amazing, given the steep climb. She was breathing hard, but he suspected it was because she was angry, not winded.

Her cheeks were flushed with color, her eyes ice-blue darts that, because they reminded him a little of Cat's, pierced him right through the heart.

"Come on," he said, crushing the impression, replacing it with memorized snippets from the tabloid article he'd read describing the police investigation into Willa Walters's drug habits. "You're outta here."

"The hell I am." She wrestled out of his grasp. "This is state land, open to hikers and overnight backpackers."

"Yeah, backpackers with a permit. Got one?" He smirked at her, feeling good all of a sudden, strong, in control of the situation, professional all the way. He knew it would be dark by the time they got back to their vehicles, but that was fine with him, he had a flashlight and—

"Right here." She whipped a folded yellow receipt out of the breast pocket of her long-sleeved shirt. "See for yourself. I'm every bit as entitled to be here as you are."

For a long second he just stood there, mute, looking at the folded yellow paper flapping in the wind. He snatched it out of her hand. Only local DF&G or Fish and Wildlife officials could issue permits for the reserve, and he sure as hell hadn't issued her one. The only other officer in the vicinity was—

"Barb wrote it up for me."

He swore under his breath, mentally counting to ten. The next time he saw Barb Maguire he was going to drag her by that kinky black hair of hers down to the creek behind the station and drown her. He checked the dates and the signature on the receipt, confirming the worst, then slapped it back into Wendy's waiting hand.

"You can't stop me, you know. I'm going to find those caribou, and when I do find them, I'm going to photograph them. And then I'm going to get out of here." She glared up at him, her lips pressed seductively into a tight little rose.

He didn't want to admit it, but she was right. He couldn't stop her. This was state land, and she had a valid access permit. The only way to stop her now would be to judge her incompetent or unprepared. He had the authority to do it, against her will, if it came to that.

"Why did you come after me?"

The question caught him off guard. He ignored it.

He'd been thinking about just how competent and prepared she actually seemed to be.

An old but expensive compass hung from her neck by a nylon cord. Her topographic map was expertly folded into the kind of configuration a seasoned hiker would use and was protected by a plastic cover, peeking out from an easily reachable overhead pocket on her pack.

Though the backpack itself was a blinding electric blue—that's how he'd spotted her so easily—and was ridiculously big for her petite frame, it was high quality, as was her down sleeping bag, her tent and the short ice ax hanging from a loop near her liter-size water bottle.

"You're probably not going to need that," he said, nodding toward the ax.

"It's August," she shot back. "And this is Alaska. You have to be prepared for everything."

He shrugged but had to hand it to her. She was in good shape, was well equipped and had managed, so far, not to get herself lost or killed.

"You didn't answer my question."

"Hmm?" He caught himself staring at her mouth. Her lips had relaxed again, and she'd wet them unconsciously with her tongue.

"Why…are…you…here?" Enunciating each word, Wendy pantomimed sign language in his face.

He snapped to attention, irritated at himself for noticing her mouth at all, and her eyes, not to mention those cute little feet encased in top-grain leather. He wondered how her blisters were doing. "I…I'm here because you can't go in there alone, permit or no permit."

"Why not?" She stiffened, every muscle in her

face taut, daring him to come up with a reason that
would hold water.

He couldn't. At least not any reason that wouldn't
sound stupid or steeped in emotion. Like the fact that
she was a woman, alone. Whether a person was well
equipped or not, the reserve was one of the wildest,
most rugged places on the planet. There were animals, bears—

"You don't have a firearm," he said suddenly,
remembering that grizzlies might have wandered into
the northern tracts, where fishing for late-season
salmon was good.

She glanced at the forty-five holstered at his hip,
then rolled her eyes. "When was the last time you
shot an attacking bear?"

"Never." He didn't even have to think about it.
"It's never been necessary."

"Exactly," she said. "And you live here. I'll only
be here five or six days."

Again he couldn't argue, but that was beside the
point. He didn't like the thought of her out here
alone. What if she got hurt? What if something happened? It would be his fault because he didn't stop
her. Ultimately he was responsible.

He thought bitterly of Cat, and how insistent she'd
been on going to New York alone last year. He'd
wanted to go with her, but she'd argued against it,
saying he always treated her like a baby. He should
have taken charge. He should have gone with her. If
he'd only been there…

The sound of loose rocks above them snapped Joe
back to the moment. He'd buried his sister, but not
the memories. Never the memories. He would never
let himself forget. Or forgive.

"Gotta keep moving," he said. "We can't stay under the pass like this. Rock slides happen all the time up here. That shale is unstable."

"Fine." Wendy started *up* the trail.

"Whoa!"

She turned and arched a neatly plucked brow at him. "Yes?"

"You're hell-bent on this, aren't you?"

"I am."

He held his temper in check. The sky, along with his mood, was growing darker by the minute. Given the weather, what little light there was wasn't going to last much longer. He tried a different tactic.

"Fine. Have a nice trip."

Surprise registered on her face. Bingo. Maybe she'd figured all along he'd come after her. But the surprise lasted only a second, not long enough for him to bask in the momentary triumph he felt. She replaced it with a smug smile.

"You, too," she said cheerily. "Take care going back. It'll be dark soon."

The little minx! She turned to continue her climb, and it was all he could do not to grab her and…hell, he didn't know what to do with her. If she wanted to risk hypothermia, injury or worse, fine. It was her choice.

Joe spun one-eighty, nearly losing his balance on the narrow trail, and started back down the mountainside at breakneck pace. It wasn't until he'd made it all the way back down the steep approach to the pass that he saw it—a big boot print smeared across a thin streak of mud-covered rock. It hadn't been there twenty minutes ago when he'd made the climb up. He was positive.

Their mystery escort was somewhere close by. Scanning the trees below him and the rock above him, he flipped the leather trigger guard open on his revolver. Just in case.

The second time Joe caught up with her, she looked relieved.

"You're back?" Wendy said.

"Yeah. Changed my mind. I'm going with you."

"What?"

"Save it. This is my reserve, my turf. It's like you said, each of us has as much right to be here as—"

"I don't need you to baby-sit me." She did an about-face and continued up the trail.

Joe figured three days in, snap a few pictures, three days out—if she could keep up the pace. He didn't like it, not one bit, but he was resigned to it. As long as she was in his reserve, she was his responsibility.

The small, U-shaped pass, a tiny chink in the saw-toothed armor of the mountain range, was just above them now. Wendy was moving fast, too fast, and reached it a split second before he did. She let out a strangled sort of squeak.

Joe grabbed her to steady her, then eased her, backpack and all, down onto the impossibly small piece of real estate that was the pass. He sat cross-legged alongside her. "This is why it's called a 'gun-sight'." There was barely enough space for two of them in the narrow notch. "Get it?"

"Yeah," she breathed. "I do." Together they looked out over the sheer drop-off, at the densely forested valley and majestic peaks on the other side. "I had no idea it was so beautiful."

"I had no idea you were thinking of taking another swan dive into thin air." He nodded at the ground, a dizzying couple of hundred feet below them. ''Lucky for you, I was here.''

He expected a pithy comeback, and was surprised when her face softened. ''Look, I really appreciate it, okay, but honestly, I don't need your help. I don't need anyone's help. I have an assignment, I know what I'm doing and I'm going to do it. Period.''

''Don't let me stop you.''

She made a huffy little sound in the back of her throat. ''I don't intend to.''

''Good.''

''So…how do I get down?''

''You mean *we*.'' No way was he letting her go on alone. Not now. He was sure someone was following them, the same someone who had followed them yesterday, and who'd crept around outside the cabin last night.

Maybe he was overreacting. Maybe it was just another hiker. No. Intuition told him otherwise. Damn! He didn't need this. He didn't need *her* lousing up the quiet week he'd planned for himself.

Leashing his irritation, he pointed to a narrow cut in the rock to their left that angled down the cliff face to the forested valley below. ''The footing's good, but you have to watch out for slides. Lots of loose rock up here.'' He nodded toward the craggy, snow-dusted ridge above the ledgelike trail.

Wendy stared at it for a long time, as if she were deciding whether or not to go on. He was angry, but not surprised, when she pulled out her map, flattened it on her lap and positioned her compass directly over the pass on which they perched. She moved the bezel, drew a couple of transecting lines onto the map with a mechanical pencil she fished out of her pocket, then scribbled down a heading.

Joe was impressed. "You didn't learn that in Manhattan."

"No," she said. "I didn't." They stared at each other for a drawn-out moment, and he found himself wondering what she was wearing under that long-sleeved shirt. "Michigan," she said, snapping him out of his momentary lapse into insanity. "The north woods. I was raised there."

On impulse he reached out and plucked a stray twig from her hair, his gaze fixed intently on hers. She didn't flinch, nor did she break eye contact until he did.

"You're full of surprises, aren't you?"

In a voice so soft, almost as if she were talking to herself, she said, "You don't know the half of it."

Wendy argued with him as she wolfed down a Power Bar.

The battle escalated between gulps of water she felt obliged to share with him, since, in his haste to catch her, he'd forgotten his own bottle. It peaked during the risky process of shimmying into her waterproof anorak without pitching headlong into the valley below. But it was no use. Joe Peterson was as immovable as the mountain they were roosted on.

"Okay, fine. Let's go, then."

He stood and offered her a hand. "I'll help you."

She would have rather burned in hell.

"I'm fine," she managed through gritted teeth, as she struggled to her feet, her heavy pack throwing her dangerously off balance and making her feel like a pregnant turtle in a bright-blue shell.

Joe gripped her upper arm to steady her, and before she knew what she was doing she'd grabbed on to him for support. Their gazes locked, and for the barest second she thought of him sitting, bare-chested in the Adirondack chair in his bedroom, staring at the photo of his dead sister.

"Thanks," she said quietly.

"No problem." He let go of her, then motioned her out onto the ledgelike trail leading down into the wildlife reserve.

There was loose rock everywhere; the footing was precarious, at best. "Is this trail used often?" Wendy had done a lot of backpacking when she was a kid, but mostly in Michigan over flat terrain that was nothing like this.

"By animals, mostly. It's really just a game trail. Not too many people come in this way."

"I can see why." She tried not to look down as she placed one foot carefully in front of the other and made her way down the steep route.

Two switchbacks later it dawned on her. "My compass!" She stopped short, and Joe nearly ran into her.

"Whoa! What about it?"

"I left it on top, on the pass. I took it off for a minute to—"

"We'll snag it on the way back. It'll still be there."

Taking care with her footing, she turned toward him. "You don't understand. My dad gave me that compass. It's the one thing that wasn't stolen along with the rest of my stuff. I had it in my camera bag. It's important to me. I wouldn't want anything to happen to it."

Joe swore, then glanced at the sky, which looked as if it was about to explode. "We're almost out of daylight, and I don't like the looks of those clouds. Stay here."

Wendy grabbed his arm. "No, I'll go." It was her compass, and she was the one who'd left it behind.

"No, *I'll* go. Like I said, stay here."

Before she could argue, he turned and started back up the trail. "Tyrant," she said to his back, knowing he couldn't hear her.

A moment later, a spray of small rocks rained down from the jagged ridge line above, peppering the space Joe had just occupied. Wendy flattened herself against the rock face and protected her head with her hands. Sheesh. He wasn't kidding about those rock slides.

After a moment it stopped, and she cautiously looked up, expecting to see a marmot or maybe a bird, but saw neither. She also didn't see Joe. The trail was empty, and the notch in the rocks he'd called a pass was empty, too.

Below her everything was quiet, the wooded valley dark, the trail disappearing into shadows. There was no wind, not a breath of it, which seemed unusual to her. Checking her watch—8:00 p.m.—she realized that, if not for the storm clouds, there'd still be plenty of light.

Joe was right. They needed to get down from the pass and find somewhere to make camp before it got dark. Which didn't give them much time since it was nearly dark already.

"Joe?" she called up the trail, straining to see in the half light. "Did you find the compass?"

She could just make out the pass, and could see

he wasn't there. Where had he gone? She was beginning to get cold. Her anorak had a miniature temperature gauge hanging from the zipper. She drew it up close to her face, squinting in an attempt to read the tiny numbers. Forty-six degrees. Brrr. Summer in Alaska, what a treat.

"Joe?" she called again.

This time she got an answer.

Another shower of rocks let loose from above. A sharp-edged missile glanced off her temple, startling her. "Ow! What the—"

"Wendy!" It was Joe's voice, and she had to admit she was glad to hear it.

Covering her head with her hands, she started up the trail toward him.

"Hurry!"

The rock shower became more violent. She hunched over, using her backpack to shield her, and trudged upward. Something hot stung her right eye. She swiped at it with a hand, and her fingers came away wet.

"No, wait!" he called. "Go back! Wendy, go back!"

"What?" She hunkered down under an overhang, pressing herself close to the wall of rock on her right, and squinted up the trail. "Joe, I can't see you."

What she did see was—

"Oh, God."

Rock slide didn't describe it, not by a long shot.

It looked as if the whole side of the ridge had given way above her. Chunks of shale and volcanic rock pummeled the trail in a raucous staccato, bouncing and skipping off the cliff face, then the ledge, and shooting out into space.

Wendy let out a half shout, half scream, working desperately to keep her footing. She heard the tumble of rocks below her in stereo as they hit the bottom of the valley, the sound echoing off the surrounding mountains.

"I'm coming down!" Joe's voice again. "Stay where you are!"

But she couldn't stay where she was. Loose scree and dust was fast filling in the crevices between the larger rocks that had caught and held on the ledge. The trail was literally disappearing around her. A minute later and she'd be trapped under the overhang.

"Joe!" She had to move. Up was out of the question. The trail was almost gone in front of her. How would he get to her? She realized he probably wouldn't, he couldn't—not in time, anyway—and that she had to do something to save herself. Now.

Down. She had to get down.

Wendy moved, or rather crawled, backward on hands and knees, the blue backpack protecting her from the worst of the rock fall. The slide wasn't as bad in this direction. Three feet felt like three miles, but she made progress.

She knew her hands were cut, and a sticky warmth she realized was blood kept trickling into her eye. Not that she could see more than a few feet in any direction, anyway. The dust was thick as smoke.

She heard Joe somewhere above her, shouting, but she couldn't make out his words. She should try to help him, but how? What could she do? She felt helpless, useless, and *that* made her mad.

The shower of debris lightened, and as the dust began to clear, Wendy crawled forward again, calling

Joe's name, toward the overhang that had sheltered her. She felt her way upward, reaching blindly ahead of her for the next handhold.

Her scraped and bloodied palm connected, at last, with something solid.

"I've got you!" he cried, and pulled her up.

Chapter 5

"I was fine."

Joe zipped the two-man backpacker's tent closed and shot Wendy a hard look. "You were *not* fine."

Even under the harsh beam of her flashlight, cut and bruised and bloodied, and as tightly wound as she'd ever seen any man, Joe Peterson looked good to her.

And that was a bad thing.

"I'd made it down, past the rock slide. I was out of danger." She handed him the first-aid kit she'd paid $34.95 for in an Anchorage sporting goods store. "The only reason I climbed back up was to help you."

"Help *me?* Me," he said again, as if the notion were ridiculous.

"Yes."

They had, in fact, helped each other. They'd crouched together under the overhang until the danger was over, then Joe had used her ice ax as a make-shift shovel to clear the trail below them. A tiny flame of satisfaction burned inside her, knowing she'd been right and he'd been wrong about the tool coming in handy.

When the rock slide started, Joe had ditched his pack at the pass, and now there was no way to retrieve it. The trail above them had been completely destroyed. All they had in the way of gear were the contents of her pack. Lucky for him, for them both, she was prepared.

"Let me see that cut." He brushed the hair away from her face and peered at the nasty incision she'd sustained during the slide.

"I can do it," she said, and pulled away. He ignored her, pressing an iodine wipe firmly to her temple. "I said, I can—ow! That stings."

"You'll live." He held her chin and swabbed at the cut, then cleaned the dried blood from her face with some sterile cotton.

She let him do it. Why, she didn't know.

The look on his face as he performed the task was one of detached concentration, sprinkled with a dose of mild distaste. She felt like a stray mutt who'd been rescued by the local animal shelter.

"Oh, here, give me that." She snatched the cotton from him when he began to inspect the cuts on her hands. "I'm perfectly capable of cleaning myself up."

He nodded at her broken nails, the undersides of which were caked with dirt. "Manicure didn't last."

"Very funny." He was a real comedian, wasn't he?

She fished a couple of antiseptic wipes out of the

first-aid kit and went to work on her face and neck, then her hands and arms, managing to remove most of the dust and grit and dried blood. What she wouldn't give for a shower.

Now she knew what the phrase "hit by a Mack truck" really meant. Exhaustion warred with adrenaline, producing an almost euphoric state she suspected was mild shock.

Joe didn't look any better off, though she suspected a guy like him would go to his grave before he'd admit he was whipped. From the moment he'd grabbed her hand and had pulled her to safety under the overhang, he'd taken charge of the situation. He'd told her what to do, and she'd done it, without question.

But by the time they'd made their way to the bottom of the pass, him carrying her pack, and had moved a quarter mile into the cover of the trees, searching for a flat, protected spot in which to camp, Wendy had regained some of her strength and all of her convictions.

She'd refused to allow him to pitch her tent without her help. It was *her* tent, after all. He'd actually believed she'd just sit there, idle, and let him do it for her. After an argument about the proper way to filter water from a nearby creek, and after an awkward moment when she needed to relieve herself but he refused to allow her out of his sight, they'd settled in to their cramped quarters for the night.

Now he just looked beat. Exhausted. Not that she could tell by his actions or words, which, like everything else in Joe Peterson's world, were carefully controlled. But she could see it in his eyes and in his face when he thought she wasn't looking.

"You hungry?" he asked, and produced another of her Power Bars.

"No, just tired."

He ripped open the foil wrapper and downed the peanut-butter-flavored energy snack in three bites. Then he unzipped her new, goose-down sleeping bag and moved out of the way so she could climb in. "Here. Get some sleep."

Until this moment she hadn't considered the fact that there was just the one sleeping bag between them. One toothbrush, one washcloth, one everything. "What about you?"

"Don't worry about it." He grabbed the flashlight and flipped it off.

In the close-to-claustrophobic space, even in the dark she could make out his movements. He settled down beside her, his head near the opening of the tent. She heard the crisp rustle of nylon and Gore-Tex as he pulled his jacket over himself for warmth.

She knew this was the last place on earth he wanted to be—stuck in a tent in the middle of nowhere with a woman who, for a number of reasons, some valid, some not, disgusted him. But here they were, all the same, and the last time she'd checked, the temperature gauge on her anorak had read thirty-nine degrees.

Swiveling around so they were facing the same direction, Wendy unzipped her sleeping bag all the way, and lay down next to him. "We can share it," she said, and draped the open bag over them both.

"It's not necessary." He pushed it aside.

"Don't be silly, it's freezing."

He didn't protest a second time when she redistributed the bag to cover them. They lay there for a while, awake. She could tell by his breathing and by the palpable tension between them that sleep wasn't anywhere on his radar.

She'd noticed, too, that he hadn't taken his gun off. It was still in the holster secured to his belt, and poked her in the hip when she fidgeted. She was also aware that the camping spot he'd chosen for them wasn't visible from the trail, and that he'd deliberately not built a fire.

An odd recollection gnawed at her.

Barely an hour ago, right before Joe had caught up to her on the approach to the pass, she could swear someone was following her. Not Joe, but someone else, dressed in dark clothes that blended right in to their surroundings. She'd only caught a glimpse of the person. She'd stopped and had waited to see if he would emerge onto the trail, but he didn't. She wasn't even sure if the person *was* a "he," or if the whole thing was just her imagination.

"Joe?"

No answer.

"That rock slide…it was an accident, right?"

He stirred under the goose-down bag. "Go to sleep. Tomorrow's a long day."

Even if Joe were carrying a communications device—which he wasn't—she knew there was no cell phone or two-way radio coverage this far from town.

They were stuck.

"We can't go back through the pass, can we?"

He didn't answer. She turned onto her side to look at him in the dark. "Joe?"

"No," he said stiffly. "We can't go back."

She'd studied the map and knew the gun-sight pass was the only way in or out of the reserve from the east. Jagged, snowcapped peaks thousands of feet high surrounded them on three sides.

Tension balled in her stomach. She *had* to get those photos. She had to be back in New York in less than three weeks. "So…"

"The only way out is down the valley, past the caribou habitat, right through the middle of the reserve." His tone made it plain he blamed their predicament entirely on her.

She refused to let him bully her. "How long?"

Another silence. She felt his anger as if it were a living, breathing thing laying in wait between them. "Two weeks. That's if you can make it at all."

She turned her back on him and wrapped her arms around herself—not for warmth, for Joe Peterson was generating enough body heat to melt a polar ice cap—but for courage.

"I can make it," she said.

I have to make it.

Joe was used to waking up in the middle of the night, but for entirely different reasons than the one shocking him into consciousness now.

Wendy Walters was cuddling him in her sleep.

He lay on his side, turned away from her, one hand resting on the weapon strapped to his hip. Wendy was curled around him like a pretzel, one arm snaked around his torso, a leg pinned snugly between his. He could feel her breasts pressed up against his back, the soft weight of them as they rose and fell with each breath.

He realized he had a hard-on the size of Texas. After adjusting his trousers, he tried, without luck, to untangle himself from her. She scooted closer as he inched toward the side of the tent. In the end he jammed the sleeping bag down between them, so at least they weren't in direct contact.

His watch read nearly six, though he didn't need it to judge the time. Gray light bled through the thin fabric of the tent. This time of year it got dark around nine and light again around five.

He hadn't meant to fall asleep, but there'd been no fighting it. He'd barely gotten a couple of hours the night before at the station. He'd lain there in the tent, awake, as long as he could, listening, waiting to see if they were going to have more company.

He was sure, now, that they were being tracked, followed. Not they, so much as *she*. Wendy. He was also sure that rock slide was no accident. It was meant to separate the two of them, to get her alone.

The question was, who was the guy following her and what did he want?

Joe hadn't seen anyone on top of the pass when he'd hiked back up to retrieve Wendy's compass, but he'd had a weird feeling that someone was there, hiding above them between the pinnacles of broken, snow-dusted rock. The same someone who'd made the boot print he'd seen where the wooded canyon below them met the steep approach to the pass.

After the slide had started, out of the corner of his eye he'd seen movement above them, a familiar flash of predator-gray camouflage. He would have gone after the guy if it hadn't meant leaving Wendy alone. Moreover, seconds into the slide, Joe had known the trail wouldn't hold. He had to get to her or risk being separated. And like it or not, Wendy Walters was his responsibility, it was his job to keep her safe.

That's what he made himself believe in the gray

light of dawn, her heat at his back, the scent of her on the goose-down bag covering them. He told himself that was the only reason he'd dumped his pack in a panic and had scrambled down the trail, desperate to reach her.

Wendy sighed in her sleep and snuggled closer. Joe had nowhere to go. He was trapped between her and the wall of the tent. He'd edged off his half of the inflatable pad beneath them, and now the only thing between him and the hard, frigid ground was a few millimeters of rip-stop nylon.

Twenty seconds later he was up and out of the tent.

It was annoyingly clear to Wendy after nearly half an hour of arguing, during which time they'd boiled water for tea using her single-burner backpacker's stove, shared a breakfast bar and repacked her gear, that Joe Peterson was never in a million years going to let her carry her own backpack while he carried nothing.

"Okay, fine," she said at last. "You carry it."

She pulled the old knapsack she used as a camera bag out of the blue pack, and slung it over her shoulder. Her Nikon was already strapped securely to her chest in a professional harness, loaded with film and ready to go. The snowcapped peaks surrounding the reserve were beautiful, and small wildlife was abundant. She intended to get some good shots today regardless of the weather, which looked iffy, at best.

She'd slept like the dead and felt good this morning, almost guiltily so. Joe had made it plain, not with words but with cold looks and abrupt movements, that he was not happy about having to spend the next two weeks with her.

Too bad. She refused to feel guilty. That slide was no more her fault than his.

"Ready?" he said, as he cinched the belt of her blue backpack tight across his hips.

"Ready."

"Okay, I'm only going to say this once. If you want to get out of this in one piece, you'll do exactly as I say, exactly when I say it, no questions asked. Got it?"

She looked at him, conscious of the fact that her mouth was hanging open and both brows were raised to the ten-thousand-foot level.

The old Wendy, Blake Barrett's girl Friday, would have quietly nodded compliance, would have stepped into line behind him and followed his lead.

"You're kidding, right?"

The slight tic at the edge of his mouth and the intensity of his eyes, which had gone a dark hazel rimmed with gold, told her he was dead serious.

She reminded herself that, regardless of the painful similarities of character, Joe Peterson was not Blake Barrett, and even if he were, she was not the same Wendy Walters she'd been a month ago.

"You know what, Warden?" She crossed in front of him, moving onto the trail and taking the lead. "I've already had one controlling bastard try to run my life, I don't need another."

She started down the trail and heard his heavy footfalls as he stepped into line behind her. A smile bloomed on her face.

"Did it ever occur to you that people, controlling

bastards included, sometimes do things for your own good?''

She snorted and picked up the pace.

''That maybe, just maybe, they know better than you do what to do in certain situ—''

''No,'' she said, cutting him off. ''I can make my own decisions.''

The trail snaked downward into the long, densely wooded valley that ran the length of the reserve. It bordered the caribou habitat some forty miles ahead of them. She had a map, supplies, and knew exactly where she was going. It was comforting to know that she didn't need Joe Peterson's help, even if he was hell-bent on her accepting it.

''Seems to me, *Willa,* some of those decisions didn't turn out to be too smart.''

The way he said her old name, the thinly veiled reference to the lies he'd read about her in the tabloids, made her stop short and turn on him.

''You don't know anything about me or what really happened. You have no right to judge me based on a pack of lies you read, just because—'' She stopped herself before she went too far.

''Because what?'' He stood close to her, too close, and looked down at her, his expression now one of calm confidence. A man in control.

God, he was good-looking. That should have been the last thing on her mind, but there it was.

''Because...'' Their gazes locked, and for a second she read something overtly sexual in the way those eyes of his drank her in. It scared her a little.

Which didn't say much for her experience with men. Although she'd been around lots of them, she was woefully undereducated in the romance department. Not that Joe Peterson had romance on his mind. Far from it.

She'd been close to saying that he had no business judging her just because his sister had died of a drug overdose. She was glad she'd stopped herself. He was acting like a jerk, but she didn't have it in her to twist the knife.

"Who was the guy?" he said abruptly.

"What guy?"

"The controlling bastard? The other one, I mean."

She almost laughed, and felt the tension in her shoulders uncoil itself. He'd actually made a joke. It wasn't particularly funny, but it had diffused the situation, which, she guessed, was his intent.

"Just somebody I used to work with."

"Oh. I thought maybe he was your husband or your ex, or somebody like that."

She caught something else in his eyes, then. Something she couldn't quite discern.

"No, nothing like that. He was my boss."

"Oh." The something cooled, but didn't entirely disappear. "You were sleeping with him."

She didn't even dignify that with a response. Turning on her heel, she started forward again, down the trail.

"Whoa!" He grabbed her arm, stopped her. "Cool your jets a minute." She was about to bite his head off when he said, "The trail's washed out in a few places, and we'll need to hike cross-country. If you're going to lead today, you'll need this."

He fished an object out of the pocket of his shirt and handed it to her.

"My compass!"

"It was right where you said it was, on top of the pass."

She looked at the worn tick marks etched on the beat-up plastic bezel and remembered for a breath when it was new and her father had given it to her.

"Thanks," she said, trying hard to conceal her delight.

"No problem." They stood there for a long uncomfortable moment looking at each other. Then a branch snapped behind them, and Joe spun in the direction of the sound.

His hand moved lightning fast to the gun holstered at his hip. Statue still, they stood silent for nearly a minute, peering back up the trail, but nothing appeared, not even a squirrel or a bird. His gaze swept the woods on either side of them.

"What is it?" she whispered.

He shrugged, but she could tell from the tightness of his expression, from the stiff way he moved, that he knew more than he was telling. "Nothing," he said. "Let's go."

Two hours later they stopped for a drink and to refill their shared water bottle at the stream roaring down the valley beside the trail.

Wendy pointed to a small boxlike symbol on her topographic map, eight or so miles ahead of them. She knew it signified a building or other man-made structure. "What's this?"

Joe handed her the full water bottle and took the map from her. "Department of Fish and Game cabin. There're a half dozen of them in the reserve along the main trail." He pointed to the others, which were spread out between Joe's station and where they were now. "They're open to the public in the summer, by reservation only."

"That's great! Any reservations this week?"

Joe gave up a huff, which was as close as she'd seen him come to a laugh all day. "Not likely. We don't get too many visitors here. Too far off the beaten path."

"That's why you like it here, isn't it?"

"Maybe."

There were no maybes about it in her mind.

She said, "At least we won't have to spend another night together in that tent. It was a little…crowded, don't you think?"

Joe looked at her with what she'd come to recognize as cool amusement. "Yeah, you could say that."

She distinctly remembered waking up in the middle of the night and finding his arm around her. She'd managed to move it without waking him.

"What are we going to do about food? I only brought enough for myself for a week. And now there are two of us, and we'll be out here for two weeks."

She glanced speculatively at the rushing water of the stream beside the trail, and wished she'd invested in a lightweight, telescoping fishing rod at the sporting goods store.

Joe read her mind. "Don't tell me you fish?"

"Of course I fish. Well, I used to."

"Michigan again?"

"That's right." She could tell from his expression that this new bit of information surprised him.

"Daddy teach you?"

"No." She arched a brow at him. "I learned in Girl Scouts."

"You were a Girl Scout?" He did laugh then. "You?"

"Yes, me. I was a Girl Scout. Six years, in fact. Is that so hard to believe?" His preconceived notions about her were becoming irritating. She plucked her camera bag from the ground and started toward the trail.

"How many badges you get?"

"What?" She tried to tune him out.

"You know, badges. Fire building, cooking, hiking, first aid, the works. There're about fifty different ones, right?"

She glanced back at him, but kept walking. "How do you know about stuff like that?" He didn't answer, and then it dawned on her. "Was Cat a Girl Scout?"

They walked another twenty yards before he answered. "She was, for a year or so, but it wasn't really her thing."

"You were the outdoor type, but she wasn't."

"Something like that."

He didn't say any more about it, and she thought it best to change the subject. "So, what are we going to do for food?" She had visions of using dental floss as fishing line, and of him shooting squirrels with his revolver.

"I keep a stash of emergency supplies locked up in each of the cabins along the trail. Just in case."

"In case you get stuck hiking a hundred miles with a wildlife photographer who only brought enough Power Bars and beef jerky to last a week?"

"Yeah. Happens all the time out here."

She smiled, despite her determination not to like him. She'd kill to know what he was thinking, and was tempted to look back at him, but didn't.

As they made their way down the valley, storm clouds darkening the sky above them, the scent of spruce infusing the cold air, spurring her onward, Wendy had to admit she was glad Joe Peterson was with her.

Chapter 6

She reacted as if they'd just checked into a suite at the Captain Cook, Anchorage's best hotel.

"This is great!"

Joe grunted, closed the door of the rustic A-frame cabin behind them and eased out of Wendy's backpack, which he'd carried for the past twelve miles. It wasn't that he wasn't in shape, it was just that the pack was too small for him. His back and shoulders ached like hell.

"It has everything!" Wendy swept the beam of her flashlight across the spartan interior of the Department of Fish and Game cabin. "Potbelly stove, two sets of bunk beds, firewood, a snow shovel, the works! Look, there's even a loft."

"Yeah, it's plush, all right." Joe dug in his pants pocket for a set of keys. Wendy watched as he opened the locked closet that ran the length of the cabin's far wall.

"Blankets!" she said.

"And food and clothes. Even some cooking gear." A razor, too, he thought, running a hand over the two-day growth of stubble on his chin. And my own damned toothbrush. He'd borrowed hers that morning.

He pulled the unisex toiletries kit from the closet and tossed it to her. She handed him the flashlight, and he rummaged around inside the closet until he found what he was looking for.

"Propane lantern?"

"Yeah. I'll just fire it up and we can—"

"I'll do it." Wendy snatched it out of his hand. A minute later she had it going.

"Don't tell me," he said. "Girl Scouts."

"What? Oh, no...the, uh, directions are printed right on it. See?" She pointed at the white enamel lettering on the side of the lantern.

Standing there smiling, fists bunched on slim hips, she looked so fresh and alive and...spunky was the word he was looking for, as if they'd just been for a Sunday stroll in the park instead of a twelve-mile hike through a remote wilderness.

He had a hard time reconciling this Wendy Walters with the woman portrayed in that tabloid. He had an even harder time convincing himself he wasn't attracted to her.

"Hungry?"

"Hmm? Oh, yeah. Starved."

She pulled a foil-wrapped, freeze-dried dinner from the backpack. "Chicken à la king. Perfect. I'll cook."

He built a fire in the stove, then rolled out her sleeping bag on one of the wooden bunks. On the opposite bunk, for himself, he tossed a set of old blankets from the closet. There'd be no snuggling tonight.

He watched as Wendy set up her backpacker's stove on the floor between the bunks. There wasn't a table in this particular cabin. There wasn't room.

Her ingenuity surprised him. In addition to the chicken à la king, which required only boiling water to prepare, she managed to make biscuits on the potbelly stove, out of what had to be year-old old Bisquick she found in a sealed tin in the closet, a metal pan and an improvised oven she constructed out of tents of tin foil.

Joe was impressed.

When they sat down to eat, cross-legged on a blanket on the floor in front of the stove, he asked the question he'd been wanting to ask for two days.

"This…guy, your boss. Barrett or whatever his name is."

Wendy put her fork down. "How do you know his name? I never mentioned it."

"It was in the article." Which was true. Blake Barrett had been mentioned in the tabloid article, but only as an aside. Joe wouldn't have put two and two together if Wendy's editor at the magazine hadn't mentioned him, too.

That snake didn't even have the decency to speak to the police on her behalf.

"He wouldn't be out here looking for you, by any chance, would he?"

Wendy looked at him hard. "What makes you say that?"

He shrugged. "No reason." He didn't see any point in scaring her.

If Barrett was the guy following them—and Joe was one hundred percent sure *someone* was following them, though there'd been no sign of their camo-clad escort since the incident at the pass—he would deal with him himself. That rock slide could have killed all three of them.

Wendy looked at him suspiciously, her brows pinched together as if she were trying to read his thoughts. "Is there something you're not telling me?"

"No." He shoveled another forkful of the chicken à la king into his mouth. "Not bad for freeze-dried."

She scrutinized him for a moment, and while he knew she didn't take his answer at face value, her shoulders finally relaxed and she continued eating. He noticed, not for the first time, how delicate her features were. Small face, pointed chin. A mouth like a piece of ripe fruit.

He liked her eyes, they were big, almost too big for her face, and were framed by a fringe of dark lashes. They lent her an air of innocence he knew was only an illusion, but that he found damned attractive all the same.

He wondered if her blunt-cut blond hair had come out of a bottle. He didn't think so, but you never knew these days. It was mind-blowing what women did to themselves in the name of fashion. His sister used to spend hours in the bathroom styling her hair and doing her makeup. Then again, fashion had been Cat's business. An ugly business. It had been Wendy Walters's chosen career, too, he reminded himself.

He watched her as she set her plate aside and grabbed her Nikon off the bunk where she'd placed it when they'd come in. Throughout the day she'd stopped along the trail to take pictures. At first he'd protested, because he thought they'd fall behind and not make the first cabin by dark. But Wendy had proved for the third day running that she was a fit hiker in damned good shape.

He'd let her lead today, not because she'd forced the issue and he'd given in, but because he wanted to watch her back, keep an eye out for the guy tracking them. He didn't want her to fall behind, not that there seemed much chance of that given her fitness level.

"What do you do, jog or something, back in New York?" He'd seen a dozen movies where urban types ran for exercise, through Central Park and around some cemented-in reservoir.

"Hmm?" She glanced up from her camera, a roll of spent film in one hand, and caught him looking at her legs.

"You're in pretty good shape. What do you do to stay fit?"

"Oh." A blush washed her cheeks. "Yeah, I try to run every day. Well…on days when I'm not hiking across miles of Alaskan wilderness." She smiled at him, and it struck him how pretty she really was, in a Meg Ryan, girl-next-door sort of way. Which, again, didn't fit.

She loaded a fresh roll of film into her camera with an economy of motion that told him she'd done it thousands of times, could do it in her sleep. She tossed the spent roll into a deep pocket of the ratty green knapsack she used as a camera bag.

"All set for tomorrow," she said, then grabbed her map.

They studied it together, which required him to

move closer to her. He could smell the faint scent of shampoo—his shampoo from the station—in her hair. There was something about her using his shampoo, his soap, taking a shower in his house, sleeping there, that he liked.

And that bothered him.

"We probably should get some sleep," she said, aware of his eyes on her.

"Yeah." Shaking off her effect on him, he jumped up and cleared away their supper dishes.

Twenty minutes later, after they'd made a final trip outside to the outhouse the DF&G had installed the previous year, and after he'd secured the cabin, Joe stoked the fire in the potbelly stove and left its cast-iron door hanging open for warmth. Wendy killed the lantern, and the room was at once bathed in a soft orange light.

Settling in on the bunk opposite hers, Joe looked away as she shimmied out of her khaki trousers. He listened to her wrestling with her clothes for another minute, then, unable to stop himself, he sneaked a peek, and caught her sitting there in nothing but her long-sleeved shirt. He glimpsed a flash of white panties as she swung bare legs onto the bunk, then noticed her bra folded neatly on top of her pants on the floor.

"Good night," she said, oblivious to his spying, and burrowed down inside her sleeping bag.

Pulling the emergency stash of blankets over himself, he watched the firelight dance off the cabin's rustic beams. "G'night."

Later, drowsy and at the edge of sleep, Joe heard the swoosh of nylon as Wendy turned in her bag.

"Just for the record," she said. "Blake and I...we weren't lovers."

* * *

The next day the weather was clear, but it had rained hard overnight and the trail was muddy and slick, completely washed-out in some places. Wendy noticed that the stream rushing beside them grew wider and more violent, more like a river, the farther they hiked down the valley into the reserve.

Around noon they took a break, with barely four miles under their belts. Downed trees and thick undergrowth had made for slow going, and she'd stopped at several places along the way to take photographs. Mostly birds and small game. They hadn't seen any bears or moose or any of the larger animals that lived in the reserve. And, to her disappointment, there'd been no sign of the elusive woodland caribou.

Joe had insisted on walking behind her, and she noticed that *he* noticed and reacted to everything with caution—every sound, every print in the muddy trail—as if he was expecting to see something, or someone. She hadn't had that weird feeling, as she'd had the day before yesterday, that someone was following them. But Joe had it. She could tell.

"Want your jacket?" he asked, as he slipped out of the blue backpack and propped it against a tree.

Despite her protests, he'd taken the pack apart that morning and had widened the adjustable frame to fit him. She'd argued that, since the pack fit *her,* as is, she should carry it. Naturally, he hadn't agreed. In the end she'd made him promise to readjust it again before they parted ways.

"Sure," she said, taking her anorak from him. "Thanks."

Though blue sky was visible through the thick

canopy of spruce above them, the temperature was
only in the low fifties—typical for an Alaskan summer—and Wendy felt chilled. Everything around
them was wet, and icy water dripped from the trees.
She donned the waterproof anorak and instantly felt
warmer.

Over the past day they'd settled into a polite but
cool sort of camaraderie, resigned to the fact that
they were going to be spending the better part of the
next two weeks together, twenty-four seven.

Wendy watched as Joe stripped off his department-issue shirt, then dug around in the pack for
what she suspected was the thermal undershirt he'd
salvaged from the emergency supply closet at the
cabin they'd slept in last night.

When he found it, he set it aside and pulled his
T-shirt off over his head. Standing there in the
woods, sun filtering through the trees, catching in the
tawny-gold hair of his chest and highlighting the
sculpted muscles of his arms and back, he looked
like a primeval man.

The calm stoic features of his face, that strong jaw-
line and long straight nose moved through alternating
bands of shadow and light as he wrestled himself into
the thermal.

Before Wendy realized what she was doing, she'd
popped the lens cover off her Nikon and had snapped
some photos in quick succession.

"What the—" He pulled the shirt down over his
torso, and flashed cold green eyes at her. "What do
you think you're doing?"

"I—" Her reaction had been pure instinct. She
was a photographer, for God's sake. A men's fashion

photographer. Or at least she had been, and old habits die hard. "I was just taking your picture. The trees, the light, it was all so perfect. I wasn't thinking, I was just—"

"I'm not one of your boy-toy models." He snatched his green overshirt from where he'd set it and threw it on, misbuttoning it, then he restuffed items into the backpack.

"I know you're not. I didn't mean it that way. It was just that you looked so—"

"What?"

For the barest second she remembered him sneaking a look at her last night when she was half-undressed. He hadn't known she was aware of him, that she'd deliberately let him look. Her attraction to him scared her. She didn't need this, not now, not with a guy like him.

"Oh, hell, why am I explaining myself to you?" She snapped the lens cover back on the camera and grabbed her knapsack.

She was done with explaining, with feeling guilty or sorry or suffering angst over the million little things she'd been made to feel were her fault in her seven years as Blake's assistant. She was also done with reactive, domineering alpha males.

"There's a bridge up ahead we have to cross," he said icily. "No telling what condition it'll be in after these storms. Let's roll."

"Fine." She moved in front of him and started down the trail, determined not to let Joe Peterson get to her, then promptly lost her footing in the mud.

Joe grabbed her elbow. "Slow down, the trail's slick."

"I don't need your help."

"Suit yourself, then." He let her go, and again she nearly lost her footing.

"Wh-which way?" Clumsily she righted herself, working to keep her anger in check.

There was a fork in the trail. One spur led down to the river, which had grown to a raging torrent. The other snaked up the side of the heavily wooded valley.

"Up there. See it?" Joe pointed.

"See what?" She started up the trail, not waiting for him to answer.

A few minutes of hard hiking later, during which she lost her footing no fewer than four times in the slippery, rock-laced mud, she saw what Joe had been pointing at.

"This is the bridge?" Wendy felt her eyes widen to saucer size.

"Yeah, this is it." He moved up behind her and poked her in the back. "Let's go."

"You're kidding, right?" He had to be. What she was staring at, openmouthed now, like a trout, was *not* a bridge. At least not her definition of a bridge. It was a serviceable catwalk, maybe, or a prop from a Tarzan movie, but a bridge it was not.

"Nope, no joke. That's the only way across. Unless you've got wings stashed in that camera bag."

Her stomach did a flip-flop. "But, it's so narrow."

"It works. Come on." He edged around her and climbed the last few feet up to the flat area blasted into the rock that served as the anchor point for the hundred-foot-long suspension bridge spanning the frothy torrent below them. "Besides, you've already managed two death-defying experiences in as many days. This'll be a cakewalk in comparison."

Now that she was over the initial shock of it, she could see he was right. Heights didn't bother her, and she had decent balance. She looked at the bridge, a tightly constructed walkway of steel, thick cabling and wood. "All right. I'll go first."

"Not a chance. See those wooden slats?" He nodded at the walkway. "They're wet, and slicker than you-know-what. You'll slip and break your neck. We'll go together."

Though the sun was high, it was cold, and she could see that indeed the slats were wet, some of them still icy from the morning. All the same, his attitude—this mind-set that she was stupid, helpless without him—was really beginning to irritate her.

She arched a brow at him, gesturing to the small sign fastened to the steel anchor point that read, "Caution: Only one person at a time allowed on bridge."

"Yeah, yeah, but that's not because of weight. The damned thing buckles like a roller coaster when you get a bunch of people on it single file."

The bridge was too narrow to traverse two abreast. What, did he think he was going to carry her across?

"Like I said, I'll go first." Stepping in front of him she grabbed the cables on both sides. Before she could launch herself onto the walkway, Joe grabbed her around the waist.

"You'll fall." He looked her in the eyes, his face inches from hers, so close she felt his breath on her face. "We're going together."

The arrogant bastard!

His hands were like brands around her waist, his gaze burned hotter. For the barest second she thought about what it would be like to kiss him, to run her tongue around the inside of his mouth.

She could swear he read her mind.

A millisecond later she wrestled free of him and launched herself onto the bridge.

"Wendy, no!"

But she was too quick for him. To her supreme satisfaction, she got away and jogged nearly twenty feet across the slick wooden slats, sheer momentum keeping her upright. The walkway pitched and rolled under her weight. She stopped short, grabbing onto the cabling for support, and waited for it to still.

Looking back, she saw Joe, his teeth gritted behind tightly pressed lips, his eyes dark points of heat that burned into her—a man seeing red, but maintaining his cool. A man in control. Oh, yes, was he ever. He hadn't dared to step onto the bridge after her. His weight and movement would have caused it to pitch more wildly than it already had from her abrupt getaway.

"See," she said. "I'm fine."

He didn't say a word. He just stood there, glaring at her. It was good for him, she thought. Good for him to be forced into allowing someone to determine their own destiny without his constant intervention. Good for him to realize that Wendy Walters, the *new and improved* Wendy Walters, could take care of herself, thank you very much.

She inched backward on the walkway, one foot, then the other, sliding her hands along the cabling, still looking at him.

It was good for her, too. To realize that she *could* take care of herself, that she didn't need a man telling her what to do every second of the day. She definitely didn't need Joe Peterson fawning over her as if she were—

"Stop!" He bolted toward her, onto the bridge, his gaze narrowing past her.

The walkway rolled. She glanced behind her and saw what he'd seen. Too late. His weight caused a swell the size of a tsunami. She slipped and landed hard, vaguely aware of Joe letting loose with a couple of choice swear words.

The next thing she knew she was sitting on the bridge, grabbing for the cabling, one leg plunging between two icy slats, one of which had come loose from the walkway and was dangling free over the river below them.

"If you'd waited until I'd gotten across, everything would've been fine."

Joe dropped his pack onto the wet ground on the other side of the suspension bridge and dug around inside it for the first-aid kit. "Yeah, just dandy. So now it's *my* fault."

"Yes, it's your fault. It's entirely your fault." Wendy sat gingerly on the waterproof tarp he'd spread on the ground for her, then rolled up her pants leg. "I wouldn't have fallen if you hadn't come after me."

"If I hadn't come after you, you'd be dead now." The thought of it made his gut clench.

Their gazes locked. She knew he was right, but wouldn't admit it. She was the most stubborn, pig-headed…

"Here." He pushed his warring thoughts and ridiculous emotions aside, and tossed her the first-aid kit.

"You're bleeding, too." She nodded at his right forearm. "There, where the frayed cable cut you."

"It's nothing."

"It's not nothing. Come here, let me see it."

He shrugged off her help. "Deal with that scrape on your leg, and I'll see to myself."

"Fine."

They spent a few minutes doctoring their own wounds, which were minor, considering what could have happened. Wendy had slipped through a broken slat on the walkway, sustaining a scraped calf that he suspected didn't sting nearly as badly as her behind, which had landed hard on the walkway when she'd fallen.

He spent a second thinking about that behind. A second too long.

"What now, Warden?" She looked at him as if he were the one responsible for her current state.

Which he was, he reminded himself.

What had happened today had completely reinforced his world view.

"We've lost too much time today already, and the trail conditions are bad. No use trying to reach the next cabin. We'll log a couple more miles, if you're up to it, then make camp for the night."

She looked at him as if he'd suggested they stand on their heads and sing. "We've got to keep moving! If we don't make better time, if we don't reach the caribou habitat soon, I'll never get my photos and get back to New York before the magazine's deadline."

Joe shook his head in disbelief. The woman nearly buys it, and all she can think about is getting her damned snapshots. She was something else, all right.

"That's not my problem," he said, zipping the first-aid kit and tossing it into the pack. "What *is* my problem is getting you out of here. Alive." He got to his feet and offered her a hand.

"So it's the tent again, tonight."

"That's right." His hand remained outstretched, waiting for her to take it. With pursed lips and a resigned look on her face, she did, and he helped her up.

Only after they'd made camp for the night, a few miles down the trail, once she was safe and warm and he was by her side, did he allow himself to relive the panic that had punched him in the gut when he'd watched her take that fall.

Only, he was the one falling.

Falling hard, for a woman who ran with the kinds of scum and lived the sort of lifestyle that had gotten his sister killed.

It was time he knew what he was dealing with.

"There's something we need to talk about," he said, propping himself up on one elbow in the tent so he could look her right in the eyes.

Wendy rolled toward him in her sleeping bag. The flashlight was perched on top of her boot in the far corner, and lit her face only peripherally. "What?"

"The bridge," he said.

"What about it?" Her blue eyes looked so big, so innocent, he almost believed she hadn't seen what he'd seen—or, if she had, that it hadn't registered.

"It was tampered with. That slat was deliberately cut."

Chapter 7

Wendy listened, her skin prickling, as Joe told her about the boot prints he'd seen on the trail two days ago.

"All this time someone's been following us, and you didn't tell me?" Wendy freed her arms from the sleeping bag and sat up in the tent.

"Not following us, following *you*. Come on, Wendy, you knew. You had to have known. You're not stupid."

The thing was, she *had* known. She'd felt it since her very first day in the reserve but had kept her suspicions to herself. "So, the rock slide..."

"No accident."

"And the bridge..."

Joe looked at her hard. "You saw it yourself. Six of the slats on that walkway had been partially cut so they'd hold your weight, but not mine."

"Well, they didn't hold my weight, did they?"

She recalled with a shiver how Joe had reached her and had pulled her to her feet, how they'd climbed onto the cabling of the suspension bridge and had worked their way across, avoiding the slatted walkway altogether.

Once he'd seen her safely to the other side, he'd backtracked to close and lock the gate at the far end of the bridge, so that other innocent hikers in the area—if there were any—wouldn't cross. On his way back he'd knocked out the rest of the damaged slats, leaving a gaping hole in the bridge that highlighted the long fall to the boiling river below.

"This guy obviously wants you alone. Those *accidents* were meant to separate us."

A light rain pinged against the waterproof nylon of the tent. Wendy felt suddenly chilled and pulled the goose-down sleeping bag around her shoulders.

"What I want to know, is why? Who's the guy, Wendy?"

She looked at him, not attempting to hide her surprise. "How should I know?"

His eyes sharpened to points.

"Wait a minute…" she said. No way was she going to let him turn this around on her. "Before we get to that, let's go back to the part where you knew about this mystery guy and you didn't tell me. What were you thinking?"

His stony expression didn't change. "That I'd take care of it."

"Just like that, you'd take care of it."

"That's right."

She threw off the sleeping bag and scooted toward him, close enough so their knees were touching, close enough to grab the front of his Warden Rambo shirt and shake him. "Let me get this straight. Someone's following *me,* and not only do you not tell me about it, you decide, without consulting me, that *you're* going to take care of it." She glanced briefly at his holstered handgun. "Whatever that means."

He started to defend his actions, but she wasn't listening. Her teeth ground together behind her lips, her hands balled to fists in her lap.

This was exactly the kind of thing Blake would do. Keep information from her, make important decisions concerning her without her input or knowledge. Anger bloomed inside her like a poison flower. Then she remembered the reason Blake had run her life.

She'd let him.

Her fists relaxed. A long breath eased from her lungs, and with it she let go her sudden rage.

"You saw this guy, didn't you?" Joe said.

She looked at him, really looked at him, at the way his eyes softened, the way his face tightened in concern, and realized he was just trying to help her.

"Yeah." All the fight had gone out of her. "I thought I saw him a couple of times."

"Christ, Wendy, why didn't you say anything?"

Why hadn't she?

Covering herself with the down bag, she pulled her knees up to her chest, then wrapped her arms around her legs in a bear hug. "I don't know."

It was a lie. She did know.

She'd been afraid to tell him, because it would have meant telling him everything.

"It's cards-on-the-table time, Wendy." Joe forced her to meet his gaze again. "Who is this guy?"

"Honestly, I don't know!" Which was the truth.

She had no idea who this maniac was. Hey, wait a minute… "Why would I have to know him? Maybe he's just some kook who gets his kicks terrorizing women."

"Yeah, right. Out here, a million miles from nowhere. I don't think so."

He was right. Not only did that scenario not make sense, she knew in her gut that this mystery man, whoever he was, had singled her out, purposely. But why?

"Tell me again about your stolen luggage."

She shrugged. "There's nothing to tell. Some guy—I didn't get a good look at him—just grabbed it off the conveyor and ran."

"What was in it?"

"Nothing." She shook her head. "Clothes, toiletries, some old camping gear from my folks' place in Michigan. Just the usual stuff."

She felt uncomfortable under his scrutiny and let her gaze drift to the play of the flashlight beam on the walls of the tent.

Joe grabbed her arm, roughly enough to startle her, and recaptured her attention. "What aren't you telling me?"

A lot.

But that wasn't the answer she gave him.

A week after the incident in the Manhattan loft, her purse had been snatched. Three days later her apartment was burglarized. At the time, she hadn't connected the two incidents, nor had she really thought all that much about them, since she was spending nearly every waking hour either talking to the police about what had happened with the male model, fighting off tabloid reporters or trying to reach Blake, who'd refused to see her.

"Back off," she said to him, and pulled her arm from his grasp. "Who put you in charge of my life?"

"You did, the second you stepped into this reserve."

Ouch.

She smirked at him but couldn't argue. She knew that, regardless of her own choices or actions, Joe Peterson felt responsible for her as long as she was on his turf. He was more than ready and willing to "take care of things" as he'd put it.

And in the end that's what she feared most of all.

That's why she hadn't told him about the other incidents, or about the man in the dark clothes she'd glimpsed near the trail two days ago.

Joe's rugged good looks, the obvious physical attraction between them, his strength of character, the concern he tried, but failed, to mask behind that stony expression of his...all of it, taken together, set off cautionary alarms inside her.

It would be far too easy to lean on a man like him, to let him take over, make her decisions, solve her problems for her. She'd done that once already, and with disastrous results.

Wendy shook her head.

She'd been young, too young, and Blake's urban sophistication, his self-confidence and power, his charm, all of it had sucked her in. But she wasn't a naive twenty-two-year-old anymore, and Joe Peterson wasn't Blake Barrett.

"Your sister," she said, remembering that Cat Peterson had been just twenty-two when she died. "You two were close?"

The question caught him totally off guard, but he didn't look away. Back at the station, when she'd asked him about Cat, he'd become angry and had retreated. But now they were in a four-by-eight tent with nothing but a sleeping bag between them, and there was nowhere for Joe Peterson to go.

"Not really." He shrugged. "She was a lot younger. It's just that…"

He did look away then, but Wendy knew he wasn't finished. She could see it in eyes, in the way his muscles bunched and how he absently massaged the back of his neck.

"Our parents died when I was twenty-one. Cat was only twelve at the time."

Wendy had to stop herself from saying she was sorry. Joe didn't want her sympathy. He would have hated it, in fact. What he wanted, needed, she suspected, was simply to talk about it.

"I'd just finished college, just started at DF&G. So I moved her in with me."

"You raised her," Wendy said, not trying to hide her admiration.

Joe shrugged. "It wasn't so hard."

"I don't believe that for a second. Teenage girls are a handful. I know. I was one."

He shot her a half smile. "Yeah, I'll bet."

"Wasn't there anyone else, an aunt, an uncle, another relative who could've taken her?"

"Sure. But she was my sister. She was *my* responsibility. No way was I farming her out."

Wendy wasn't surprised by this admission. In fact, she would've been stunned had he answered her question any other way.

"It must've been pretty tough on you. A young guy with a kid sister tagging along."

He shrugged.

"You must've missed a lot. You know...parties, girls, that kind of thing."

"I was never much into parties." His gaze washed over her in a way that made her suddenly overwarm.

"You never...married or anything?"

"No." Their gazes connected. "You?"

Wendy shook her head. "No. Never even been close."

"That's hard to believe."

She held his gaze and thought about what it would be like to kiss him, to make love to him, to wake up with his arms around her in the morning.

As if he'd read her mind, he quickly looked away.

Pulling the sleeping bag up to her chin, Wendy shook off the thought and focused on the topic. "So, then, Cat—"

"What is this, twenty questions?"

His abrupt change in temperament surprised her.

He pulled a couple of blankets from the blue pack and tossed them onto the tent floor. "She was a damned nightmare, if you want to know the truth." He yanked off his boots and chucked them violently into a corner.

Wendy was stunned. "Your sister?"

"Yeah. A real pain." Looking for something else to take out his sudden aggression on, he punched a pile of clothes into a makeshift pillow.

"Once, up at the lake, before Mom and Dad died, Cat stole the neighbors' canoe and took it out on the water. With six or seven kids in it!" He flopped down on the blankets and slammed his head into the pile of clothes. "It capsized, of course. All the kids could swim. All of them except Cat."

"You saved her," Wendy said, guessing.

"Damned right, I did." He flashed angry eyes at her. "Of all the stupid, lamebrained…"

"She was just a kid. Kids do stuff like that."

"She almost drowned."

"But you saved her."

Joe sat up, launched himself at her, stopping just short of touching her. Wendy went stock-still. Their faces were inches apart.

"Don't you get it? She could've been killed. She made a stupid decision that nearly cost her her life."

"But you were there. You—"

"What if I hadn't been? It's just like…*this.*" He waved his arms in the air. "The rock slide, the bridge. You should have listened to me, damn it! You should never have come out here on your own."

"Hey, wait a minute!" She threw off the sleeping bag and scooted closer, until they were nose to nose.

"What if I hadn't come after you?"

"I'm not a child, Joe."

His gaze washed over her breasts, loose beneath her T-shirt, then fixed for a moment on her mouth. "I can see that."

They looked at each other and, behind the anger, Wendy read raw desire in his eyes, a palpable sexuality she felt beneath the skin.

"And…and you're not my big brother." She backed off, and so did he, but their eyes remained locked.

"No," he said quietly. "No, I'm not."

It rained all night.

The next morning they woke up cold and wet, the bottom of their tent soaked. Two hours, barely three miles, into the day's hike, which was painfully slow going due to the mud and enough downed tree limbs to feed a lumber mill, they reached the second cabin.

"There it is," Joe said and pointed up the trail to a clearing.

"Thank God. My boots are so wet they squish." Wendy picked up her pace and made for the cabin.

Before she reached the clearing, he caught her arm. "Hang on. Let me check it out first."

He stepped in front of her, flicking the leather trigger guard off his handgun, which, for now, he kept holstered. Scanning the surrounding woods for movement, he moved cautiously toward the cabin. Water sluiced down his face. He swiped at his eyes, narrowing his gaze over the steep, forested ridge above the cabin.

Wendy followed. "Is he…still with us?"

Joe had neither seen nor heard any signs of their mystery escort since yesterday's mishap on the bridge. Still… "Oh, yeah. He's out there."

Trepidation clouded her eyes, and he was aware—though she wasn't—of her edging closer to him, close enough for him to put his arm around her.

Which he did. "Come on. Let's get inside."

The cabin hadn't been disturbed since the last time he'd visited it, about a month ago on a regular reconnaissance hike into the reserve. It was a little larger than the last cabin, and better furnished.

Wendy set her camera bag on the table. "I'm glad we stopped. It'll take me just a few minutes to get into some dry clothes and change my socks. Want some lunch before we head out?"

"Head out? You mean keep going?"

"Of course." She stripped off her anorak and shook it out next to the door. "We've got the whole rest of the day. If we pick up the pace, we could make another eight or nine miles before—"

"Whoa. Hang on a second, hotshot. We're not going anywhere."

"What do you mean?" Her brows pinched together in a frown. "We've got at least nine hours of daylight. Even with the rain, and the sky as dark as it is, we could—"

"No." Joe plucked the wet anorak from her hands and tossed it onto on a peg on the wall. He shrugged out of his soaking jacket, which he hung next to it. "The trail's sure to be washed out between here and the next cabin. We'd be knee-deep in mud inside an hour." He nodded at her feet. "Look at your boots. Hell, look at my boots."

Despite waterproof clothing and high-quality leather hiking boots, both of them were soaked to the skin, and he knew from the sky and from experience that this storm was with them to stay.

"I'm nearly out of time here, Joe. It's been four days and we've only come what, twenty-four miles?"

"Twenty-five. In bad weather and with somebody on our tail who wants us stopped." Or dead, but he didn't say that. He didn't want to scare her any more than was necessary.

She pulled her map out of the camera bag and smoothed it on the table. Gray light from the cabin's only window provided enough illumination for them to see. "The caribou habitat's here." She pointed to the spot on the map he'd shown her four days ago.

"We're here, a good fifteen miles away. And then we've got to hike out—the long way!"

"And your point is?" He knew what her answer would be, but he was in the mood for a fight.

He'd never met anyone like her. She just wouldn't give up. He'd known that about her from the moment they met, when he'd held his gun on her and she'd looked him in the eyes and told him to put that thing away.

"I need those photos, Joe. I need them now, and I need to get my butt back to New York."

"Your butt—" he gave it an appreciative glance "—isn't going anywhere. Not today it's not."

She reached for the blue pack, intending, he knew, to put it on. He read angry determination in her eyes. She was looking for a fight, too, but she damned sure had to know he'd never let her go on without him.

Mustering his control, he placed a hand around her upper arm, then squeezed.

She shot him a deadly look.

"Okay, I want you to listen to me."

A blond brow arched in one of her "go ahead, I'm waiting" looks.

He almost smiled. "I know how important getting those photos is to you." He remembered the conversation he'd had with her editor.

She's desperate, trying to start over, make a new life for herself. Getting away from Blake Barrett was the smartest thing she's ever done.

"But there's one thing more important than those photos. More important to me, anyway."

"What?" Her tone and the way she looked down her nose at him even though he was nearly a foot taller than she, warned him she was ready to disagree with whatever answer he gave her.

"Your life."

Surprise flashed in her eyes.

He loosened his grip on her arm, but was struck by how warm she was, even wet, through the thin fabric of her shirt.

"There's a guy out there who's dangerous. Under normal circumstances I'd go after him. But the circumstances aren't normal."

"You mean you've got me to think about."

"That's right."

Her expression softened. "Okay, I buy that. Even though I told you before that—"

"Yeah, yeah...you don't need a baby-sitter. You don't get it, Wendy. It wouldn't matter who you are. Man, woman, Barb Maguire's dog, whoever—I'm an officer of the state, sworn to serve and protect. This is my reserve and you're in it."

They stood there, looking at each other, and he watched as a change came over her face.

"So...I could be anybody, and you'd be doing this. Protecting me."

"That's right." He slid his hand down her arm, but didn't let go.

What he didn't tell her, what he didn't want to believe, was that she wasn't just anybody. Not to him. She was under his skin. Big-time. And Joe Peterson had a bad feeling she was there to stay.

Just after midnight he moved silently along the perimeter of the clearing, moving from tree to tree, the steady rain drowning the sucking sounds his military-style boots made in the mud as he approached the cabin.

His piece was shoved into the waistband of his camouflage dungarees, pressing at the small of his back, but he didn't plan to use it, not tonight. He wanted her alone. It would be easier that way.

They hadn't paid him enough to kill the son of a bitch playing bodyguard. Oh, but he wanted to. He smiled, remembering the last time, a couple of weeks ago in New York. It hadn't been in the game plan, but he'd done it all the same.

And he'd liked it.

Listening hard, he waited a full five minutes before peeking into the cabin's window. When he did, what he saw surprised the hell out of him. A fire burned low in the metal stove, giving off just enough light to see her.

Curled up on a single bunk inside her sleeping bag, Willa Walters was…*alone*. Imagine that. Hero Boy was sprawled in the bunk opposite, his face turned to the wall. The dimwit wasn't getting any, after all.

Scanning the interior, his gaze fixed on an old green knapsack, the bitch's camera bag.

"Soon," he whispered, changing his focus to the blond's mouth. Her lips parted seductively in sleep. "Oh, yeah. Very very soon."

Chapter 8

Both of them saw the boot prints in the mud outside the cabin the next morning.

Wendy didn't say a word.

"Starting today, right now, our number-one objective is to get back to the station as fast as possible. Got it?"

She stared at the waffle-pattern impressions under the window, and for the first time was truly scared.

Her near-accident that first day, the rock slide at the pass, the incident on the bridge…her fear reaction to those events had been instinctive, the whoosh of adrenaline completely natural.

But this…the feeling she had now, this tightening in her stomach was entirely different, the furthest thing from natural she could imagine. Nothing in her experience prepared her for this kind of fear.

"Let's go," Joe said, and nodded toward the washed-out trail.

He'd been right about the storm. It was with them to stay. Their wet boots and clothes had dried overnight next to the fire. Good thing, too, because the temperature was five degrees colder this morning than it had been the same time yesterday. The rain had turned to sleet, and Wendy knew enough about Alaska to know that, even in August, it could turn to snow.

Joe had also been right about the trail. She could see that now, as she picked her way carefully over downed limbs and a minefield of washed-out potholes filled with frozen mud. Yesterday afternoon those same potholes would not have been frozen, and it would've been dead easy to take a wrong step, twisting an ankle in the process.

She hated to admit it, but she was glad, now, that he'd forced the issue and she'd eventually given in to his demand to overnight at the cabin. Maybe she'd overreacted to his bad behavior, his need for control. Now that she knew the real scoop on his sister, she understood his motivations—even though she didn't agree with them.

"It was smart of you to pack that waterproof sealant," he said, bringing her back to the present.

This morning she'd retrieved the small tube from her pack, and they'd rubbed a thick layer of it into their dry boots.

"Are you actually complimenting me?" She shot him a look over her shoulder. Maybe he was beginning to think she wasn't completely helpless after all.

"Yeah, I guess I am."

A smile bloomed on her face. She made sure he didn't see it.

The going was tough, but she moved at a brisk

pace up the valley with Joe in sync two steps behind her. Yesterday's rest had done them both good. She felt renewed, strong, ready for the long day they intended to put in.

"You remember what I told you," he said, right behind her.

"Of course I do. Watch my footing, but watch the surroundings, too." The trail ahead of them, the dark stands of trees on both sides. Be aware, he'd said.

"Any movement, anything out of the ordinary you see or hear or feel, you stop. Understand?"

"Yes." She wasn't about to argue. Someone was with them, either ahead of them or behind them, every step of the way.

Joe wanted her in front of him so he could watch her back. The thought of it gave her a little thrill. Not because he was watching her, so much as watching out for her, protecting her. Which was something no man had ever done for her since she'd left home at eighteen.

She knew, too, that what they were doing—running—wasn't natural for a man like Joe. In a choice between fleeing or fighting, Joe Peterson would choose the fight every time. Not this time, though. This time he had her to think about. Something about it made her feel warm inside, despite the weather.

She wore her Nikon under her anorak, ready to go should they see any signs of woodland caribou. Joe had made it clear they were making for the station as fast as humanly possible, and she agreed with that plan to a point.

Their trail ran right alongside the caribou habitat Joe had shown her on the map, and if she'd judged the distance correctly, they'd reach it by early to-morrow at the latest.

She intended to be ready.

"How you doing?" he said.

"Fine. Good."

"How're those blisters?"

She'd doctored them a couple of times in the past few days. "They're okay. The moleskin's working like a charm."

"Good."

Her cuts and bruises were healing, too, as were his, from what she could see of them. The two of them looked like anybody else, average hikers, not two people on the run from someone dangerous.

"What about you?" she said.

She'd noticed that despite the fact that he was used to backpacking and hiking long distances on patrol, he seemed to be having trouble keeping up with her. It was the blue pack. It was stuffed to the gills with her equipment, extra food and emergency supplies he'd rifled from the last two cabins.

"I'm okay," he said.

She topped a small rise and stopped to let him catch his breath, then watched him as he readjusted his load, taking a minute to scan the tree line in every direction.

On impulse, Wendy reached for the heavy tripod sticking out of the top of the pack. "Here, let me carry that. I can attach it to my knapsack easy."

She'd left its black case behind in the SUV, opt-ing, instead, to house it in a light waterproof bag that would fit in the pack.

"No way. I can manage." Joe stepped out of reach.

"You're being ridiculous. I'm not carrying anything, just lenses and film. My knapsack's practically empty."

"I said I can manage." He recinched the padded waist belt of the pack, emphasizing the fact that he wasn't about to share his load with her.

She could have embarrassed him by pointing out that he was the one barely keeping up, that he was the one breathing hard now that the trail was steeper. But she didn't.

Instead she arched a brow at him. "Look, whether we want to be or not, we're in this thing together, right?"

"So?"

"So…that makes us a team."

He snorted.

"Well, doesn't it?"

He looked at her as if he already knew where she was headed with her argument, and he wasn't happy about it.

"You want me to listen to you when you think you're right, don't you?"

"Yeah. I do." His voice was as icy as the needles of sleet stinging their hands and faces.

"And I'm prepared to do it." She reached for the tripod again, and this time he didn't back away. "As long as you listen to me when *I'm* right."

He grabbed her arm and she froze, eyeing him, her brow arching higher as if to say, "Well, Warden, what's it going to be?"

She could see him mentally struggling with the idea of her helping him. In that sense, he was light-years different from Blake. Her former boss and mentor had been notorious for saddling her with not only her share of the load, but his, as well.

"Come on, Joe," she said quietly, "let's work together on this."

Slowly he let go her arm, his gaze still pinned to hers. She thought, for the hundredth time in the past six days, how great his eyes were. Green flecked with gold.

After removing the tripod from the pack, she handed it to him. "Help me, will you?" She turned her back to him so he could see the two loops she'd sewn on her knapsack to hold the tripod. A minute later she felt the familiar weight of it against her back.

"Like that?" he said.

She shot him a small smile. "Just like that. Thanks." She moved in front of him, ready to go, and waited while he readjusted the blue pack. "Better?"

Their gazes locked, and she read an uncomfortable resistance in his eyes, as if they'd crossed into territory foreign to him.

"Yeah," he said, at last. "Better."

Ten miles, two changes of socks and an inch of slushy snow later, they reached the next cabin.

Almost.

"How the heck do we get to it?" In the fading light, Wendy squinted against the sleet at the tiny DF&G cabin perched on a slab of basalt on the other side of what Joe had come to consider his own little private nightmare.

"This happens every time there's a storm and the river jumps its bank."

They both stared at what amounted to a new tributary, a frothing, boiling ten feet of water that separated them from what promised to be a warm, dry place to eat and to catch a good night's sleep—if they could get to it.

"Is it deep?" Wendy eyed the water speculatively.

"No, just fast and full of debris. Rocks, downed tree limbs, all kinds of stuff beneath the surface you can't see. There's no real chance of drowning, but in a heartbeat you could slip and bust a leg if you're not careful."

"What about you?" She gave him a once-over that he caught himself enjoying. "You're not exactly Tinkerbell-light on your feet carrying that pack."

He wasn't, and they were both exhausted. He did a slow three-sixty, on the lookout for their mystery man. There'd been no sign of him all day, but Joe knew he was there, watching them. He also knew if the guy had wanted them dead, they'd already be dead. Any idiot with a firearm and the wherewithal to kill, could have accomplished it with a minimum of trouble.

But that wasn't it. The guy wanted Wendy, alive, but not bad enough to off him to get to her. He was smart and patient as hell, but so was Joe, and he didn't intend to let Wendy out of his sight until he had the bastard checked in to a nice cold cell in the State Troopers' holding tank back in town.

"Okay," he said, dragging his attention back to the problem at hand. "This is what we're going to do…"

But Wendy wasn't listening. While he'd been thinking about their escort, she'd evidently hatched a plan of her own to cross the water. No way was it going to work.

"This is the narrowest part, right here." She pointed to a place he wouldn't cross even if he wasn't wearing a pack that weighed close to sixty pounds.

"Uh-uh," he said, shaking his head. "It's too deep there, too many rocks."

"That's the point. Some of them are huge, and look pretty stable. If we go slow, and—"

"No freaking way." He shot her a look that said he was going to have to kill her this time if she didn't listen to him.

"Look." She pointed to the closest rock, submerged only an inch or so below the water's surface. "That one right there. And there's the next one." Her gaze traveled in a snaking pattern from rock to rock. He watched her as she planned each step in her mind.

"There's got to be a better spot."

"No, I've already looked. This is it."

"We'll go together, then."

She frowned at him. "How?"

"I'll wade through the water, and help you from rock to rock."

"Don't be silly. You'll get soaked. Besides, with that pack on, you're more likely to fall helping me cross than crossing yourself." She stepped to the edge.

"No. I'll leave the pack here and come back for it later." He secured a hand around her upper arm, remembering the incident at the bridge where she'd defied him.

He didn't like the idea of leaving her alone on the

other side of the water, unprotected, while he retrieved the pack. On the other hand, he had a gun, he was a damned good shot, and was prepared to demonstrate that fact if he had to.

"Your boots will never dry by tomorrow. We can each cross on our own." He started to argue, but she cut him off. "Can't you trust me, Joe, just once, to take care of myself?"

It wasn't her words but the way she looked at him—almost as if she felt sorry for him, as if he was the one who was difficult, who was the problem in the equation—that finally broke his resolve.

Maybe he *was* the problem.

"Okay," he said, wiping the sleet from his eyes and looking at her hard. "But be careful, damn it."

"I intend to." She shot him a smile, and he thought again about how pretty she was, her cheeks rosy from cold, how her blue eyes didn't so much reflect light as were lit from within. "Wish me luck," she said, and leaped.

Joe's gut clenched. A heartbeat later she landed on the first rock, struggling for balance, her arms outstretched like a tightrope walker.

"I did it! See, it was easy."

"Yeah, you were great," he said, recovering his composure. "Just don't quit your day job."

She glanced back at him. "This *is* my day job, remember? I'm a wildlife photographer."

"Right. I forgot."

She smirked, then turned her attention back to the water rushing all around her, lapping up against the sides of her newly waterproofed boots.

As she made her way across the tributary, leaping from rock to rock, he thought about the things he'd read about her in the tabloid article recounting the drug overdose death of that male model.

None of it added up.

Hosting lavish sex parties, procuring illegal drugs, covering up evidence, lying to the police. The sordid picture the reporter had painted of Willa Walters was nothing even remotely like the woman who now held his attention.

He wondered how much of it was true, whether any of it was true. And if it wasn't, why the hell she hadn't said something. When he'd alluded to some of the things printed about her, she hadn't bothered to defend herself, not with specifics.

The question was *Why?*

He knew she was keeping something from him, but he also knew he couldn't force the truth from her. Watching her traverse the water, his stomach twisting in knots for fear she'd slip or take a wrong step, he realized he didn't want to force her. What he wanted was for her to trust him. And maybe, in order for that to happen, he needed to trust her, too.

"Made it!" she shouted when she reached the opposite side. The smile she tossed him did him in. "Now you!"

He redistributed the weight of the pack high on his hips, cinching the padded belt tight, and stepped from the muddy trail onto the first rock. As he crossed, faster and more recklessly than he should have, drawn by the magnetism of her smile, he asked himself whether he could forgive her if all the things he'd read about her in the article turned out to be true. He was thinking that it mattered, as if it were possible for there to be something between them.

When he reached the other side, he nearly lost his

footing in the mud. She placed her hands on his chest to steady him. "We did it!"

The sleet had turned to snow, and her smile faded as he moved closer and, with his thumb, brushed a flake from her lower lip.

"Yeah," he said, and kissed her.

She'd known he was going to do it, she'd seen it in his eyes before it happened. It was the single most exciting kiss of her life.

Joe's rough hands cupped her face. She melted into him, closed her eyes and kissed him back. The sound of rushing water, the solid feel of his chest beneath her hands, for a moment all of it seemed surreal. Then a slow, honeyed heat suffused her body as she felt the gentle dart of his tongue inside her mouth.

"Joe," she breathed against his lips.

He deepened the kiss, and she responded, ignoring the tiny alarms going off in her head. When his hands moved to her waist, pulling her closer, pressing her into him, she couldn't ignore them anymore.

"I...I can't do this." She broke the kiss, backed away, raising her hands in a defensive gesture meant to stop him.

It did.

"Wendy."

She shook her head, not looking at him. "Let's just get inside." Turning, she trudged up the short rise to the cabin and waited for him to get his keys out to unlock the door.

Once they were in, she buzzed about the cabin in a frenzied automatic pilot, lighting the lantern, building a fire in the stove, shucking wet outerwear, assembling items for dinner. Anything so she wouldn't have to look at him or think about what had just happened.

"Stop it," he said, and grabbed her arm.

She froze in place, water dripping from her hair onto the floor in a steady beat that made her all too aware of how long she stood there, not looking at him, saying nothing.

"Wendy, I didn't mean to—"

"It was a mistake." Tentatively she met his gaze. "We can't do this, Joe. *I* can't do it."

"Why not?" His eyes softened rather than sharpened, which surprised her, along with the gentleness of his voice. For the first time Warden Peterson, control freak, wasn't demanding an answer. Joe Peterson, the man who'd just rocked her world, was simply asking.

She sat down on one of the bunks that were standard equipment in the string of DF&G cabins they were destined to share for the next week, and thought about how to answer.

In the end she found she couldn't.

"I have too many things on my mind now. There's a lot at stake for me. Can you understand that?" It was a cop-out, but she wasn't ready to bare her soul to him.

Looking at him sitting across from her, pushing wet hair from his face in a gesture she knew stemmed from frustration, Wendy had to fight to keep her mouth shut, to keep from crossing the four-foot space separating them and collapsing into his arms.

She wanted to do it, more than anything.

"You mean your assignment. The caribou photos."

"Yes." Suddenly chilled, she eased out of her boots and swung her tired legs onto the bunk, pulling her sleeping bag around her. "I don't actually work for the magazine. Not yet, anyway."

"Yeah, I know."

"You know?" She looked at him. "How?"

He shrugged. "I talked to your friend, that editor."

"Crystal? When?" She sat up. "Where?"

"At the station, about ten minutes after you left with Barb."

"What did she say?"

"Not much. Just that you'd cut a deal with the owner or somebody—"

"The editorial director."

"Yeah, that's the guy. That he'd give you a permanent job at the magazine if you delivered the photos."

Wendy felt her lips thinning over her teeth. She was going to have a long, one-sided talk with Crystal when she got back to New York. "What else did she tell you?"

"Nothing. That was it."

She wondered if he was lying. Oh, hell, what did it matter what he did or didn't know? What did it matter what he thought about her? She rolled over, away from his searching eyes, and covered herself with the down bag.

He didn't say any more, and neither did she. She listened to him move around the cabin, checking the fire, pulling gear out of the pack, and a few minutes later smelled something good.

"Freeze-dried chili mac," he said. "Want some?"

"No, you go ahead."

"Come on, eat something. You did ten miles to-day, hard ones. You need to eat."

In her head, she counted off the miles they'd hiked over the past five days, and knew they were close to the place on the map Joe had said the woodland caribou would be. She prayed to God he was right.

"Okay," she said, and threw off the down bag. If she was going to get her photos and hike out of here in one piece, she needed to eat something. "Maybe our friend gave up," she said, as she joined him at a small table flanking the wood-burning stove.

"He's here." Joe shoveled a forkful of chili mac into his mouth. "Somewhere close."

She shivered, thinking about it.

"Cold?" He tossed her his fleece pullover, the one he'd just taken off. "Go ahead. I don't need it."

She put it on and immediately felt better. It was still warm from his body. It smelled like him, and she thought again of his mind-blowing kiss. His gaze caught hers for a split second, and she knew he was thinking about it, too.

They ate in silence after that, and she tried to un-wind, let her thoughts go, her fears, draw in the heat from the fire and strength from their supper, which turned out to be pretty darned good. She was hungry, after all.

They stayed up another two hours or so, looking at maps, reading some books on natural history and a couple of trail guides that had been left in the cabin. The whole time he never tried to touch her again or talk about what had happened between them, and she was grateful for it.

Only later, when they were both in bed on opposite sides of the tiny cabin, listening to the fire crackle and spit, watching its golden reflection dance on the walls, did she allow herself to think again about Joe Peterson's kiss and what it meant.

She realized that she did care what he thought of her. She didn't want him to go on believing she was the kind of person the tabloids said she was. She wanted him to know that, despite her chosen profession, she'd never led the kind of wild lifestyle he thought was responsible for his sister's tragic death.

She wanted him to know, but still she was afraid that in the knowing another barrier between them would fall. And right now, given her vulnerable state, she needed all the barriers she could muster.

But in the end she told him.

"It wasn't me in the loft that night," she said calmly. "It was Blake."

Chapter 9

"Tell me everything." Joe handed Wendy a mug of hot tea and sat across from her at the table. He'd stoked the fire, and its shimmering light caught in her hair, bathing her face in its soft radiance.

"It's...complicated," she said.

"Start from the beginning." He didn't want to press her, but he also couldn't just let things alone. Not anymore. He was invested in the outcome. Some guy was after her, and he needed to know who and why.

"I was asleep."

"Where? In the loft?"

"No. Of course not! At home. The phone rang in the middle of the night. It was Blake."

"So you weren't even there?" Damned tabloids. He should have known not to believe any of what had been written about her.

"I went there, to the loft. After he called."

Joe's throat hitched. "Go on."

Wendy took a deep breath. "Blake was in a panic on the phone. He said Billy—that was the model—had had a heart attack. Billy Ehrenberg was Mr. Popularity. Everybody liked him, though he led a pretty wild life. Too wild, if you know what I mean."

He remembered some of Cat's so-called friends in New York. "Yeah, I get the picture."

"Anyway, Blake wanted me over there, fast. He was crying on the phone. I'd never seen him fall apart like this. He was always so stoic, so in control." She shrugged. "What could I do? I went."

"Did he call 911?"

"No. I did after I got there. Blake was a wreck, shaking, wailing. He'd completely lost it."

"So the guy was dead when you got there."

"No. He was alive, but unconscious. He was… they'd been…" She met his gaze and held it. "I guess they were lovers. I had no idea."

Joe felt the tension in his shoulders ease. She wasn't involved. She hadn't even been there. He told himself it shouldn't matter whether she was or wasn't, because there was never going to be anything between them, anyway.

"Why did the papers say you were the one with Billy if it was really Blake?"

She looked away, into the fire, and he knew her well enough after six days to know she was embarrassed. "Because that's what I told the paramedics when they got there."

"What?" He couldn't believe it. "Why would you do that?"

Her cheeks blazed, and it wasn't from the heat of the fire. She looked at him. "Because I was stupid.

Because Blake begged me to say I was the one with Billy and not him." She lifted her shoulders. "He's married, two kids."

"And his wife didn't know about his...extra-marital activities."

"No. She's a really nice woman. I've always liked her, and kind of feel sorry for her." He started to ask another question, but she cut him off. "There's more to it than that, though."

"Go on."

"Blake is hugely successful, but recently he made a lot of investments. I think they went bad, and now he's struggling financially. He went on and on about it that night. How his wife couldn't know he was there, how he had to protect his marriage."

But not because he cared about her or his two kids, Joe guessed. The more he heard about this guy, the more he hated him. "The wife. She has money, right?"

"Exactly. Old money, from an inheritance. Years ago she funded Blake's start in the business."

"And if she found out about his shenanigans, she'd divorce him, cut him off."

"Yes. But at the time, I didn't put two and two together. I really thought he cared about her. I thought he was trying to protect her and the kids."

"Yeah. He sounds like a great guy."

Wendy looked away. "I made a mistake, okay. Plus, Blake said I owed it to him. That he was the one who taught me the business, gave me a job, kept me working when other photographers were being laid off. I owed him."

"You believe that?"

"I did at the time. Not anymore."

The guy had really done a number on her head. "What about the drugs?"

"I didn't know about that. No one did. Not for days. Blake took off, and I waited with Billy until the ambulance arrived. I went with him to the hospital, to make sure he was going to be okay."

"But he wasn't okay."

"No." She fiddled nervously with the fabric of his pullover, which she was still wearing. He liked seeing her in it. "Billy Ehrenberg died later that night."

"And still you stuck to the story that it was you and not Blake."

She nodded. "He begged me. He was desperate. And I was stupid. God, was I ever." She stood and warmed her hands over the potbelly stove. Shaking her head, she said, "Never again. Never again will I allow someone to manipulate me like that. Never."

He reached for her hand, but she pulled away. "Please don't touch me."

She was wound tighter than a Swiss watch. He wanted to hold her, to tell her everything was going to be okay, but she didn't want that from him. He backed off and just let her talk.

"Over the next couple of days all kinds of rumors were flying around about what had gone on that night. Weird sex—I mean really weird. Drugs. The whole nine yards. Reporters started showing up at my door, at work. Blake left town without a word, and I didn't know how to reach him. The whole thing just spun out of control."

"You lied to the police."

"The paramedics told them I was the one with Billy. I just didn't refute it. The official E.R. report was a heart attack, after…sex." She shrugged. "I told you. I was stupid. I just let the lie stand that it was me and not Blake.''

''And then?''

''A week later the police were at my door. Billy's autopsy report came back positive for drugs. The official cause of death was listed as an overdose.''

Joe's stomach clenched. He still had a copy of Cat's autopsy report, her death certificate. If he closed his eyes, he'd still be able to see the ink on the page.

''I'm so sorry,'' Wendy said, and unexpectedly placed a hand on his shoulder. ''You don't want to hear this.''

''No.'' He shook off her well-intended sympathy. ''I do want to hear it. All of it. Go on.''

''Okay.'' She sat down again, across from him, and looked him in the eyes. ''The second I learned about the drugs, I told the police everything, that it was Blake all the time, that I wasn't even there when it happened.''

''And...?''

''At first they didn't believe me. And by the time they did, it didn't matter. The tabloids had gotten hold of the story and...well, you know the rest.''

''Yeah.'' New York Fashion Photographer Willa Walters Overexposed in Deadly Sex/Drug Scandal. ''I know the rest.''

She took a deep breath, closed her eyes and rolled her head first to one side, then the other. ''A few days later I finally reached Blake. He denied any knowledge of the drugs. He told me Billy must have taken them before he arrived at the loft.''

''And you believed him.''

''Blake can be very convincing.''

"I'll bet."

"I did believe him. I guess I needed to. If he was lying, it would have meant that he'd used me in the worst of ways. What I started to realize was that he'd always used me, from the very beginning, to his own advantage. It was his career, not mine, that flourished in the seven years I spent as his assistant."

"What happened next?"

"Blake fired me, on the spot, when he found out I told the police the truth. He said I'd betrayed him."

"Bastard." Joe hoped it was Blake Barrett who was tracking them. He couldn't wait to get his hands on him.

"A bigger one than you can imagine. A couple of days later I went to the office to clear out my stuff and ran into Blake's new assistant—a young protégé he'd had his eye on for months. We started talking about Billy Ehrenberg's drug overdose, about how tragic it all was."

She stopped talking and looked into the fire. He perceived a struggle going on in her mind, a brittle sort of confusion twisting her delicate features. Then her expression suddenly cleared and, when she looked at him, anger flashed in her eyes.

"Blake's new girl made a point of telling me that Blake not only had access to drugs like the one that had killed Billy, but that he used them himself all the time. Oh, and wasn't I stupid not to have known that?"

"I hate this guy. I swear to God, if he's the one following us, if he so much as touches you—"

Wendy laughed, but their was no joy in it. "Our mystery escort has hiked nearly forty miles and has slept out in the rain every night. Blake's idea of the great outdoors is the ten feet between a taxi and the lobby of his Upper East Side condo. No way is it Blake.''

"You're sure about that?"

"Positive."

Joe let out a breath, his head spinning with new information. "What else?"

"That's it. My little chat with the new assistant was the last straw for me. I hated my life, myself and everything I'd become. A doormat for a manipulative jerk.''

He reached for her hand, and this time she let him take it. "It wasn't your fault. It was Barrett who—''

"It *was* my fault.'' She snatched her hand away. "Don't you get it? I let him use me, control me, all those years.'' She left him sitting at the table and climbed into her bunk, pulling her sleeping bag over her. "It was *my* life, Joe. I did it to myself.''

"You were young, impressionable.''

She snorted under the covers.

He got up, closed the door to the stove, and the cabin was instantly draped in darkness. He felt his way to the bunk opposite Wendy's and eased himself between the blankets.

"I'm twenty-nine, Joe. Not young and impressionable anymore. What happened in that loft, the events following it, was only a month ago.''

"It's over now. Try to get some sleep.''

But it wasn't over. Someone was after her. He needed to know more about what had happened that night—a lot more. And specifics about Blake Barrett that he knew she wasn't up to sharing. Not tonight, anyway.

The luminous dial of his watch read midnight. She

needed to sleep, and he needed to think. Tomorrow would be soon enough to find out the rest.

He slipped his forty-five out of its holster and shoved it under the pile of clothes he used as a pillow. He was ready for this guy, whoever he was.

She slept all of a few hours, but badly. Most of the night she'd tossed and turned, wondering what Joe thought of her now that he knew the truth about what had happened. She didn't know what was worse, having him believe she was into drugs and kinky sex, or having him know that she was a total loser.

She ran her fingers through her hair to comb it, and reminded herself that, regardless of what she'd done in the past, she wasn't a loser anymore.

"Almost ready?" Joe said, stuffing the last of their gear into the blue pack.

"Yeah." She adjusted the chest harness housing her Nikon, then grabbed her knapsack from the table. "Let's go."

"Wendy." His hand slid over her forearm. "Why don't we take a minute?"

"For what?" She knew he wanted to talk more about the things she'd told him last night. She'd been avoiding it since they'd gotten up, but supposed she might as well not hold anything back now. What was the point?

"Who's the guy? What happened that night that would make someone follow you all the way to Alaska?"

"Honestly, I don't know." She'd racked her brain a hundred times over, but couldn't come up with a connection between what had happened with Blake

and Billy in New York and the guy who was following them now.

"Well, think about it."

"I'll think about it while we walk." She started
to pull away, but he held on to her. His gaze washed
over her face, and her mouth went dry.

"I want to help you," he said quietly.

"I know. And I appreciate it. It's just that…" She
shrugged, trying to not think about how warm his
hand felt on her arm, how wonderful their kiss had
been. "You can't fix my life for me, Joe."

He didn't say anything, and she used the opportunity to disengage her arm and move to the door.

She thought again about her stolen purse, the bur-
glary at her apartment, her luggage, the unlocked
SUV. It occurred to her that maybe someone wasn't
after *her,* so much as something she *had.*

But what?

"Stick close to me today, understand?" They
stepped into the cold morning, and he locked the
cabin door behind them.

"I will." She couldn't get her mind off it. What
could she have that someone wanted? And what, if
anything, did it have to do with Billy's overdose or
Blake's lies?

She shook off her fears and focused on the new
day before them. The rain had stopped, though a
thick ground fog curled its way through the valley,
reminding her of the long cold fingers of a skeleton.
It gave her the creeps.

"When did you leave New York, exactly?" Joe
said as they walked alongside the tributary they'd
crossed yesterday and moved onto the trail.

"About three weeks ago. I didn't tell anyone

where I was going, not even the police. I'd lost my job, and my reputation was shot. Blake had made sure of that. You wouldn't believe the lies he told about me.''

''I'd believe it.''

''Anyway, I'd had it. I had to get out of there, go somewhere where I could think.''

''So you came here.''

''No, I went home. To Michigan. My parents' house.''

''Makes sense.''

''I was there about two weeks, during which time I called every fashion magazine and every freelance photographer in New York looking for a job. No one would hire me.''

''Barrett again.''

''You got that right. God knows what he told people about me. And the tabloid articles didn't help.''

''You could have sued the bastard and those newspapers.''

She sighed, and picked up the pace, despite the poor visibility. ''I could have, but I didn't want to wallow in it. I wanted to move forward, not backward. Start over, fresh.''

''So you called *Wilderness Unlimited*.''

''The senior editor, Crystal Chalmers, is a friend of mine. It's the chance of a lifetime for me. Wildlife photography was something I'd been interested in as a college student.''

''Why didn't you pursue it then?''

She turned and flashed him a raised eyebrow.

''Barrett.''

''He recruited me right out of school. The rest is history.''

And that's how she wanted to think of it, as history. She was a new woman, with a new chance at making something of herself, on her own. She wasn't going to let anyone stop her—not Blake, not the creep following them, not even Joe Peterson.

"So now you're determined," he said, nodding.

"Damn right, I am."

"Well I'm determined, too. To get us the hell out of here. Let's go."

She turned and started up the trail again, conscious of the fact that he was less than a step behind her, his hand on his gun. The man wasn't kidding. At every turn she glanced back at him through the fog, taking in the hard set of his jaw, those sharp eyes methodically sweeping the forest for any signs they weren't alone.

Two hours later, mist still curling around them like a shroud, they reached a fork in the trail, one that she'd marked on the map days ago. Wendy pivoted, hands on hips, steeling herself for what she knew, and had known for days, would be a battle.

"What?" Joe said, pulling up short.

"This is it."

"This is what?" He narrowed his gaze and looked past her.

"The fork." She nodded toward the steep game trail cutting a zigzag of switchbacks across the bald ridge to their right, snaking in and out of the fog.

"Uh-uh. Absolutely not. We keep moving."

"But this is why I'm here." She unsnapped her camera from the chest harness and popped the lens cap. "Up there is where I need to go." The rocky canyon on the other side of the ridge was the place

Joe had told her about—prime habitat for woodland caribou.

"That's the last place you're going." He took her by the arm, not gently, and urged her forward.

She resisted, digging her boot heels into the mud. "You can't stop me."

"The hell I can't!" He spun her around and caught her about the waist. She struggled, startled by his sudden show of strength, but he wouldn't let go. "There's a man out there. You're in danger. Get that through that thick, blond head of yours!"

He pulled her to him, and she dropped her camera. It lay in the mud, forgotten, as her hands pressed up against his chest. His heart beat wildly under her palm. His breath was hot on her face, his eyes as hard as she'd ever seen them.

"That guy wants you, Wendy. He wants you!" He shook her. Then, all at once, his expression softened.

Gently he pushed a wet strand of hair away from her face, his fingers lingering on her cheek, caressing it. Her stomach did a somersault.

This guy wants me, she thought.

A heartbeat later he kissed her.

Leaning into him, she simply gave up, went with it, surrendered to the confusion of feelings spiraling inside her. His tongue was hot glass, his hands everywhere at once. A breathy little sigh escaped her lips as he pulled her closer, close enough to feel that he meant business.

She wanted him so badly. More than anything, more than—

A sharp echoing *clack* startled them both.

Joe broke the kiss before she had a chance to do

it herself. She snatched her camera from the mud and followed his gaze to the top of the ridge. The *clack* sounded again. Then another.

Her heart nearly stopped.

On an outcrop far above them, two caribou bulls squared off, velvety antlers tangled, one against the other, engaged in a battle as old as time. The mist swirled around them like a ghostly dervish.

''Look!'' she said. ''We found them!''

Chapter 10

By the time Wendy cleaned the mud from her camera and checked her light meter, the caribou were gone. Up and over the ridge to the rocky habitat on the other side. She looked at Joe, and he responded with one of his don't-even-think-about-it looks.

"I have to do this," she said. "I'm going to do this."

She watched him as he thought about it, turning a slow circle, peering into the mist, listening hard for any signs of their pursuer.

It didn't matter to her if he wanted her to do it or not. She was doing it. She was going, with or without him. She didn't need his permission. It would be nice if he'd go with her. She wanted him with her, she realized, and that's probably why she wasn't already gone, still standing there in the mud, waiting for his reaction.

"Okay," he said, at last. "You first. Let's go."

The old Wendy would have said thank you. Thank you for letting me. She was grateful for Joe's compliance, but not the way she'd been grateful in the past with Blake, when he'd allow her a special assignment, making it clear she'd probably botch it on her own. No, that's not what she felt at all as they scaled the ridge. She was simply happy to have Joe with her, by her side, sharing the experience of a lifetime.

Just before they reached the top, he stopped her. "Let me go first and check it out."

Warden Rambo was back. She could see it in his eyes and knew it was useless to argue. Not that she wanted to argue. Someone was stalking her, and until they found out who it was and what he wanted, they needed to be extra careful.

"Okay," she said, and let him pass. "You won't scare them away, will you?"

"I'm a game warden, remember. My job is to keep track of animals. So, no, I won't scare them away. Come on, stick close."

She intended to, and gave one long look back the way they'd come, just to make sure no one was behind them. Joe had already done that, ten times if he'd done it once, but she felt the need to do it, all the same.

Who are you?

As they topped the ridge and the rocky canyon spread out before them on the other side, mist swirling up its walls, her heart sank. "They're gone!"

"Shh!" Joe placed a hand on her shoulder. "No, they're here, over there." He pointed to a craggy knob that shot up from the canyon bottom, obstructing their view. "On the other side of that. Listen."

She closed her eyes and listened, and heard the unmistakable *clack* of antlers. "You're right!"

"Of course I'm right."

They smiled at each other, and she felt warm all over. She remembered their kiss, and wanted another, but now was not the time. Peering through the mist, she narrowed her gaze on a rocky promontory directly across from where the caribou were hiding on the other side of the knob.

"Right there," she whispered, pointing. "That's where I need to be."

He nodded. "Yeah. Downwind, good visibility, and it's fairly protected. If you were careful, they wouldn't even know you were there. There's only one problem."

"What?"

He pulled her a few feet to the right to get a better view of the location, and she saw what he must have already known about before they'd come up here— a two-hundred foot drop-off, directly below the promontory. It was a situation not unlike the one she'd gotten herself into that first day, the day she met him, the day he saved her life on the cliff.

As they cautiously made their way down the ridge line toward the promontory, she realized just how narrow it was. It was really more of a ledge, protected on one side by a sheer basaltic wall, dropping off into oblivion on the other.

"No," he said. "This isn't going to work."

They stopped and listened again to the *clack* of antlers, but had no line of sight to the caribou.

"Yes, it is," she said, slipping off her knapsack and quickly changing lenses. She felt a surge of adrenaline as she stepped closer, inspecting the narrow ledge.

"It's what, two feet wide, max?" Joe shook his head. "No way. We can't go out there together, and I'm not letting you go alone."

She'd expected him to say that, and pretended he hadn't as she checked her light meter one last time. "Looks like we hauled that tripod for nothing. I won't be able to use it out there." She stripped it from her knapsack before putting it back on, then moved to the edge.

"No." Joe gripped her upper arm so tightly, she thought he'd snap the bone in two.

"Yes." She looked at him hard, and for a moment he didn't say anything.

"Let me do it, then," he blurted. "I'll take the pictures."

Her mouth dropped open before she could stop it. "You're not serious?" She shook her head as he argued the point. "No. Absolutely not. This is *my* assignment, my job. This is what I do."

"Squatting with a camera at the end of a runway while skinny chicks in thousand-dollar rags slink past you was your job, not this." He shook his head, looking at the ledge.

"Well, this is my job now. If I were anyone else, any other photographer—a guy—you wouldn't think twice. Admit it."

That stopped him. After a second he shrugged.

Now, more than ever, she was determined to do this herself, not only to secure her job at the magazine, but to prove to Joe Peterson that she could and that everything would be all right. It wasn't even that dangerous. As a kid growing up in Michigan she'd done dozens of things more reckless.

She realized that it wasn't the situation itself but the fact that Joe couldn't control it that was responsible for the fear she read in his eyes as he looked at her. She felt it in the way he gently took her hand in his and squeezed. It was shaking.

She also knew he didn't blame his sister's adolescent misadventures on her own poor judgment but on his lack of supervision and control. It was the same with her death. Though Cat Peterson had been an adult, Joe blamed her self-inflicted drug overdose on himself for not being there to stop her.

"This is my life, Joe. My decision. I'm responsible for the consequences, good and bad. Not you."

He didn't say anything, just looked at her. His hair hung in his eyes, damp from the mist, and she resisted the urge to reach up and brush it away from his face.

She knew he could physically stop her if he wanted to. She hoped it wouldn't come to that.

"You'll be careful," he said, at last.

She couldn't stop her smile. "Of course I will."

"I don't care how damned narrow that ledge is. If I so much as think you're in trouble, I'm coming out there."

"Here, hold this," she said, handing him the tripod, still smiling. "Back in a flash."

Joe wanted to laugh at her photographer's pun but couldn't. He set the tripod down and slipped off his pack, then watched, his stomach knotting, as she dropped to all fours and crawled onto the ledge.

They were above the tree line here, and visibility

was better. Mist swirled up the canyon, dark treetops spiking through its cottonlike ceiling.

He kept one eye on Wendy, the other on their surroundings, his hand on his gun. Camo Man was still out there, but he wouldn't have predicted they'd leave the main trail, and he couldn't follow them onto the ridge without being seen. All the same, Joe knew he was close. He could feel him watching, waiting to see what they'd do next.

The farther out onto the ledge Wendy crawled, the narrower it became. He forced himself to breathe. He tried to imagine her on a shoot in New York, up on one of those catwalks high above a stage. He told himself this was no different, a walk in the park for her. Still, he had to force himself not to follow her out there.

She stopped.

"What is it?"

Looking back at him, she smiled, raised a finger to her lips, signaling him to be quiet. She slipped out of her knapsack and placed it on the ledge in front of her, then unclipped her camera from its harness. He watched her as she dropped to her stomach and, on elbows and knees, crawled to the end where the ledge fell away into space.

Son of a bitch.

He was sweating now, though the last time he'd checked, the temperature was only in the forties. He watched as she raised her camera, popped the lens cap and focused on what he couldn't see but could hear.

Antlers *clacked*, more violently now, echoing off the rock walls of the canyon. Somewhere below them, out of sight, Joe knew there'd be a small gathering of caribou cows. That's what the battle was about, after all.

As he watched Wendy go to work, he realized he was engaged in a battle, too. Not with her, or with the guy following them, but with himself. He fought to remain detached, aloof, in control of the situation and his emotions.

But he was losing. Boy, was he ever.

Forgetting Camo Man for the moment, he knelt next to the ledge, captivated by Wendy's practiced movements as she shot an entire roll of film in under a minute, tossing the spent canister into her knapsack, reloading, changing lenses, then starting again.

Her calm demeanor, the intensity of her concentration was fascinating to him. This was her calling. She paused for a moment, set the camera down and just watched them.

He watched *her*.

Mist eased over the ledge, swirling around her prone form, then receded like a ghostly tide. In defiance of the weather, her cheeks warmed to a rose hue that was striking against the cool backdrop of rock and fog surrounding her.

A sharp *clack* of antlers echoed through the canyon, and she grinned, focused intently on her subjects, her eyes lit with a fire and an excitement he found riveting. She turned to him suddenly, their gazes connecting, and in that moment something happened to him, to them both.

Her smile changed. A second ago it had exuded the joy of accomplishment, of achieving what she'd set out to do. But now it was different, it was for him. And in that second when their minds connected, he knew. He just knew.

He loved her.

And there wasn't a goddamned thing he could do about it.

"Come on," she whispered, and waved him out. "There's room."

He didn't wait to be asked a second time. Moving carefully, he crawled onto the ledge behind her, inching closer until he was practically lying on top of her.

"Look!"

There they were. The caribou. Majestic, beautiful, their breath frosting the air as they squared off, one against the other. Together they watched them, and he was conscious of how warm she was lying beneath him, how natural it seemed for them to be touching.

Mist swirled upward from the canyon, shrouding the bulls in a ghostly ether. The effect was extraordinary. Even a nonphotographer type like himself could appreciate it.

Antlers *clacked.* Wendy tensed beneath him, picked up her camera and started shooting, spent another roll of film in under a minute. With a practiced hand she slapped a filter onto the lens and spent another.

When she was finished, she looked at him again. This time she wasn't smiling. He read it in her eyes a heartbeat before he knew it himself—they were going to be lovers. They were going to get off this damned rock, and with both feet on the ground he was going to kiss her.

The distant cry of a caribou cow sounded below them, sundering the moment. Without warning, the bulls vanished into the mist.

* * *

Wendy felt a giddy, almost surreal triumph she'd never before experienced in her work as a fashion photographer. Sure, she'd had successes in the past, but most had been diminished by Blake's micromanagement and his familiar mantra that she couldn't have done it without him.

She realized now that she could have. All that time, all those years, she could have been successful in her own right, on her own terms, without his or anyone's help. As she crawled backward off the ledge, dragging her camera bag, she knew she had a choice to make, here and now. She could dwell on the past, what might have been if only she'd been stronger, more confident—or she could look to the future, to what her life could be now, what *she* could make of it.

"Take my hand."

Safely off the ledge, she looked up from hands and knees and saw Joe's outstretched hand, the warmth of his eyes, the smile she'd only just started seeing today, and hesitated.

"You were great out there, a natural."

"Yeah?"

"Yeah." His open hand was still outstretched, waiting.

She looked at it for a heartbeat before taking it, then let him pull her up. When she was on her feet he didn't let go.

"Wendy."

She saw it coming this time, read the look in his eyes, felt the strength of his pulse where her fingertips rested on his wrist.

"We'd...better go." Backing away, she pretended

to look for a lost lens cap on the ground. When he followed her, she stopped and made a lot of work out of popping the spent film from her Nikon and tossing it into her camera bag.

"Wendy," he said again, approaching her.

"Gosh, look at the sky. It's clearing!" Flashing him a fake smile, she sidestepped him and started down the trail.

He stopped her. His hand on her shoulder was warm, his grip not demanding, but questioning. Turn around, she told herself. Turn around and kiss the man. Let him take you in his arms, let him touch you and make you come alive.

She wanted to. She wanted to so desperately. But if she did, what would happen? She was finally getting her life on track. This was all so unexpected, so new. *She* was new—too new—and didn't trust herself enough to make the right decisions where men where concerned. Especially where Joe Peterson was concerned.

"Look at me," he said.

Coward, a little voice whispered in her head.

"Wendy."

Fighting a volatile union of sheer panic and desire bordering on need, she shook off his hand and moved down the trail. "Don't leave the pack behind."

She kept walking, heard him gather up the rest of their gear and catch up with her. He didn't say a word and neither did she for the half hour it took them to hike back down the game trail into the wooded valley below.

She struggled to keep her mind focused on her new career, how she'd return to New York a success, the caribou photos in hand. She tried to envision what her life would be like working for the wildlife magazine. She had new projects to plan, lots to think about.

The only problem was the only thing she could think about for more than five straight seconds at a time was Joe. When they reached the bottom and merged onto the main trail, Wendy turned to face him.

He looked at her, his calm eyes and stoic expression no longer betraying any hints of what he was feeling—which was okay with her, since she didn't know what she was feeling, either.

"How far to the next cabin?" she asked.

"Not far. A couple of miles."

She wanted to tell him why she felt suddenly nervous and flighty around him. She wanted him to understand why she was fearful of getting involved with him. Especially him. His history, how he'd dealt with the tragedies in his life, the control he seemed so desperate to maintain, the warmth she knew simmered below the surface—all of it taken together scared the hell out of her.

"Good," she said. "I'm ready to pack it in."

"You did something today no one else has ever done, photographed woodland caribou in Alaska. You should be proud."

"Yeah, I guess I did. And I am." She nodded, reminding herself that she should be thinking about getting out of here, now that she'd gotten what she'd come for.

"There's a reward at the next cabin for all your hard work."

"A reward?"

He grinned. "Yeah. Of sorts. There's a bathtub."

"You're kidding?" She didn't even want to think about how long it had been since her last shower—almost a week ago at Joe's station. The two of them had gotten by, the past six days, by sharing a thin travel washcloth and the biodegradable soap she'd packed. "A bath would be fantastic."

"Don't get too excited until you see the tub. It's an old galvanized steel washtub I found up here in a storage locker last year."

"It sounds great."

"Yeah, it will be." He edged closer, the look she'd come to recognize as desire heating his eyes.

"I, uh, guess we should get moving." She stepped back needing to put distance between them.

"You okay?"

"Yes, I just…" She glanced at the thick foliage and dark stands of trees on both sides of the trail, disappearing into the wispy blanket of ground fog still clinging to the valley floor. "I need a minute, if you don't mind." She handed him her camera bag.

"Oh." He hesitated. "Sure." He turned his back, but didn't move from where he stood not an arm's length from her.

After the incident on the bridge he'd insisted that she never leave his sight, not for a minute, not even to relieve herself. At night that worked fine, especially at the DF&G cabins, which had nearby outhouses he could stand guard over while she was inside. On the trail it was a problem.

Right now she just wanted some privacy. She needed to get a grip on herself and her emotions. She needed to get away from him for just a few minutes. They'd been together twenty-four hours a day for almost a week.

She watched his back as he took off the blue pack, set it down, then started to rearrange its contents. There was a break in the vegetation behind her where the ground was muddy. He was clanging around metal fuel canisters and didn't hear her as she moved off the trail into the fog, just a half dozen feet or so, just far enough so she could clear her head.

She stopped where the trees made a natural barrier, breathing in the heady scents of wet cedar, spruce and loamy earth. What a week. Trying to relax, she decided that as long as she was here…

It took her just a few seconds to unbuckle her belt and unzip her pants.

A heartbeat later an arm shot around her waist.

A gloved hand clamped over her mouth, stifling her scream.

Chapter 11

She was going to die.

In the fog, in the middle of a wilderness area, the smell of greasy leather choking off her air. The only coherent thought that flashed in her mind was *Why?*

"Where is it?" he hissed in her ear.

The man dragged her backward into the foliage. He was big, powerful. She struggled, her legs tangling with his. Wrenching her head down, she saw a black jackboot and camouflage pants like the kind a hunter or a soldier would wear.

"Wendy?" Joe's voice sounded through the fog. "Damn it, Wendy." He realized she was gone. Thank God! "Where are you?"

"Answer him," the man said. A second later she felt the cold press of steel against her throat.

Oh, God.

"Answer him. And be smart about it." The hand over her mouth relaxed so she could speak.

"I—I'm here."

"Where?"

"Tell him you're fine," the faceless voice breathed in her ear.

She felt the sharp point of the knife pierce her throat. Tears stung her eyes. Joe! she wanted to scream, but didn't. "I'll be…just…a-another minute." The hand clamped over her mouth.

"Hurry up. I don't like it when I can't see you."

She tried to breathe but couldn't. Her skin felt clammy inside her clothes, her legs thick and useless, as if she were paralyzed.

"Where is it?" he hissed. His breath was hot, almost cloying against her cheek. With the knife he urged her head higher. His free hand began to explore. "Don't," he said, when a silent scream rose in her throat.

He searched her pockets, first the pants, then her shirt, dropping their apparently useless contents on the ground. "Where is it? He said you have it."

"H-have what?" she breathed. "Who?"

"Barrett."

"Wendy?" Joe's voice. It sounded far off to her right. He must be looking for her, but in the wrong direction.

The knife blade edged higher. Panic closed her throat, nearly made her legs give out when her captor cupped her breast.

"Nice," he breathed in her ear. "Now where is it? Here?" He squeezed.

She let out a strangled cry, and instantly felt the prick of the knife against her skin. Her arms flailed wildly in the air as he again dragged her backward and she tried to fend him off.

"Wendy!"

Any second Joe would find her.

She had to fight!

"Or maybe here?" As his sweaty hand moved into her open pants, she realized with horror he'd slipped his glove off. Callused fingers skimmed her bare skin.

Without warning he plunged into her panties.

"Joe!" Forgetting the knife, she launched herself sideways and they both went down. She fought him off, heedless of the flash of polished steel whooshing past her face as he tried to subdue her. Somewhere at the edge of her awareness she heard Joe's voice, hoarse with panic.

Her eyes connected with her captor's. They were brown, cold, determined, but in the millisecond she held his gaze, she realized he wasn't going to kill her, no matter what she did.

Her knee shot up hard to his groin. He blocked it, but the move caught him off guard long enough for her to wrestle free. The next thing she knew she was on her feet, running, tearing through the foliage, leaves slapping at her, branches clawing her face, catching her hair.

She was screaming.

And then she was in his arms.

"Joe!"

"Wendy, Jesus!" He scooped her up, his gun in his hand, and moved behind a tree. "What happened?"

It took only a second for all of it to register.

Her eyes, wide with fear, the dazed expression, her hair littered with pieces of broken twigs and leaves.

A thin rivulet of blood trickled from her throat. He noticed her clothes were disheveled, her pants unzipped and hanging from her hips, white cotton panties pushed far enough down to reveal blond pubic hair.

Joe came unglued.

He swore, spinning in circles, his weapon leveled at every tree, every breath of wind stirring the branches. Nothing stared back at him through the fog.

Wendy's hand on his arm quivered, bringing him back. He turned to her, fighting the tumult of rage and fear balling in his gut. "He hurt you. The son of a bitch hurt you."

"No," she said, swiping at the trickles of blood. He realized there were more than one. She'd obviously fought him off. "They're just scratches. He didn't mean to hurt me."

"The hell he didn't." He battled a primeval urge to crash through the wilderness, overturning rocks, uprooting trees if he had to, until he found the bastard. Never in his life had he wanted to kill a man, until now.

"H-he wanted to scare me, that was all. He wanted me a-alone to scare me."

He looked at her and worked to catch his breath. He knew he couldn't leave her to go after this guy, no matter how much he wanted to get him. He wasn't going anywhere without her. Not a foot. And she wasn't going anywhere without him.

"H-he's looking for something."

"What?"

She shook her head. "I don't know. I honestly

don't know. He said Blake told him I had it. But I have no idea what *it* is.''

"Come here," he said, and folded her into his arms. He wanted to close his eyes and just feel her, warm and safe against him, but couldn't risk it. "You have no idea what you put me through.''

She raised her head from his chest and met his gaze. "I know. I'm sorry.''

He shook his head. "It's not your fault. It's mine—and his, whoever the son of a bitch is. You get a look at him?''

"Just for a second. Mostly just his eyes. I think he might have been the guy who stole my luggage at the airport. Other than that, I don't know him.''

"You sure?''

She nodded. "And it isn't your fault. I was the one who slipped away. I wasn't thinking. I take that back, I was thinking, but not about the creep following us.''

He squeezed her tight and buried his face in her hair. "What am I going to do with you?''

"Kiss me," she said, stunning him, and raised her mouth to his. Her breath was warm, soft on his face.

He didn't give her a chance to change her mind. Trapping her lips, he tasted her, reveled in the feel of their tongues mating, felt the heat of her body against his. "When I heard you scream, I…''

He'd never felt that kind of sick panic before, not even with Cat when she was a kid or with any of the wilderness rescues he'd assisted on, and there'd been a lot of those in his career.

"I know," she whispered, reading his mind. "Me, too.''

They kissed again, more deeply this time, her arms

winding around his neck, his gun hand pressed into her back, and he knew he was in this thing way over his head.

"Come on," he said, getting a grip on himself. "Let's get out of here."

Late that afternoon they reached the next cabin. After Joe checked it out, Wendy followed him inside and collapsed onto one of the bunks. "What could it be? What is it this guy wants from me?"

Joe bolted the door closed, then snapped the heavy wooden shutter into place over the cabin's single window. There'd be no Peeping Toms tonight. Lighting the lantern they'd retrieved from an outside storage locker, he said, "We'll figure it out. But first you need to eat something. I need to eat something."

He unpacked the blue backpack, and they worked in concert to get their overnight accommodations into shape. It was almost automatic now, after a week together in the wild. He built a fire in the stove while she laid out her sleeping bag and his blankets on opposite bunks.

Briefly she wondered what he'd think if she laid them out together, side by side, on one bunk. She recalled his kisses, how good she'd felt in his arms, how safe, how right they seemed together...and promptly told herself she needed to calm down, be smart.

She wasn't thinking. She was just scared, terrified, when it came right down to it. And he was just being himself, an overprotective alpha male.

"Tuna casserole or beef stew?" He turned the aluminum packages over in his hands.

"Stew," she said as she searched the blue pack for a reasonably clean T-shirt.

In the cabin's outside storage locker she'd spotted the galvanized washtub, which he'd dragged inside. She looked longingly at the bucket of water Joe had placed on the stove to heat. She was desperate to bathe, to cleanse her body and her mind of the feel of that man's hands on her.

"Wendy? You okay?"

She nodded, pushing the horrible memories from her mind. "Just tired."

"He...he didn't hurt you?"

She knew what he meant, and read the pain in his face as he asked the question. He blamed himself for what had happened. Not her for leaving his side, not the camo-clad perpetrator, not even Blake, if, indeed, Blake was involved. He blamed himself, and she couldn't bear it.

"No," she said. "He...touched me. But no, he didn't do anything like that."

She watched the pulse point in his neck hitch, saw him grind his teeth behind creased lips. Lips she'd kissed and wanted to kiss again.

"He's looking for something he thinks I have."

"We need to figure out what it is, and where it is. Obviously he thinks you have it with you."

She knew it was time to share the rest of what she hadn't already told him. She felt guilty, and more than a little stupid, for not telling him sooner. Taking his hand, she sat down with him on one of the bunks.

"What's wrong?" he said, reading the hesitation she knew shone in her eyes.

She took a breath, then blurted it out. All of it. How her purse had been snatched while she was walking home from the police station one night, a week after the incident in the loft. How it was found by a passerby around the corner from her building, its contents miraculously intact. She told him about the break-in at her apartment three days later, and how, just a week ago, she'd found the door of her rented SUV unlocked, though she was positive she'd locked it. He already knew about the luggage.

"Jesus Christ!"

She knew he'd react like this, and she didn't blame him. Not now. She should have told him before. More than that, she should have put it all together herself, weeks ago. But she hadn't.

At first she'd been in shock over Billy Ehrenberg's death. Later she'd had to deal with Blake's lies, the autopsy findings and resulting police investigation, then losing her job, the tabloids, her parents...

Ouch. That had been hard.

Purse snatchings and break-ins happened all the time in Manhattan. She'd simply never connected them with Blake or with Billy. Now it seemed ridiculously clear they were related.

"What was taken from your apartment?"

"Nothing. It was just torn up. The police thought it was kids. There're some teenagers in my building, in trouble all the time."

"Tell me again what this creep said to you."

"'Where is it?' he said. 'He says you have it.' When I asked him who, he said, 'Barrett.'"

"Did Barrett give you anything after that night?"

"No, nothing."

"You sure?"

"Positive. He sent me a letter in care of my parents in Michigan. It was just a guess on his part that

I was there. I didn't tell anyone where I was going when I left New York, not even the police.''

"Where is it? What was in it?''

"I...don't know. I didn't open it. I didn't want to hear any more of Blake's lies, so I didn't read it.''

Stupid, she thought to herself. If only she'd read it, maybe they'd know what this was about.

"Where is it now?''

"The letter?'' She fished the tattered envelope out of her knapsack and handed it to him. "I carried it around in my camera bag for a week, unopened, and wrote some important phone numbers on the envelope.''

He slid a finger into the razored flap and said, "There's nothing inside.''

"I know. I threw the letter away, right before I left for Alaska. I kept the envelope because of the phone numbers.''

He read the postmark, dated nearly three weeks ago in New York.

"Damn! Maybe this guy is after the letter.''

"I don't think so. My purse was snatched and my apartment was broken into before I left New York, before this letter was even written.''

He looked at her and let out a breath. "We need to eat.''

She wasn't hungry but knew she had to keep her strength up. They had another sixty miles to hike to reach Joe's station. "I'll cook,'' she said, needing something to occupy her mind, even if it was just boiling water.

They ate in silence, and she knew he was allowing her time to think about what Blake could have given her that this guy wanted—why it was important enough to follow her four thousand miles, terrorize her and nearly get them killed, just to get it.

"Okay, let's go back to the beginning." Joe cleared their plates, then checked the bucket of bathwater on the stove. "You've told me everything about meeting Barrett in the loft. Everything you remember."

"All of it."

"Okay, let's start with the next day. What happened?"

She shrugged. "I left the E.R. after Billy died, about seven that morning, and went to the office. Blake showed up later. I didn't see him. He went to my cubicle while I was in the ladies' room and got his camera. One of the other assistants said he was really agitated, ranting like a crazy man when he—"

"Wait a minute. Why did he go to *your* cubicle to get *his* camera?"

"Because I had it. I'd found it in the loft that night after Blake had left, along with one of his tripods." She shrugged. "I was his assistant. Part of my job was to clean up after him."

"Yeah, that's an understatement."

She slipped her hand from his and looked away.

"So you took his camera, but he got it back."

"Yes, the next morning, just like I said. It was weird, though...I'd found it stashed in a corner of the loft. A drape was tossed over it, almost as if it was..."

"Hidden," Joe said.

Her mind rocketed into warp drive, sifting through the details of that night. And then it hit her. "Oh, my God, the film!"

She flew off the bunk, snatched her camera bag

from the table. Dropping cross-legged to the floor, in seconds she unzipped every pocket and dumped the contents into her lap. Dozens of new and exposed film canisters rolled across the hardwood planks.

Joe scooped them up and sat down beside her. "You have it."

"Yes." Rapidly she picked through the canisters, glancing at speeds and exposures. "I didn't even think about it. It's what I always do. Part of my job is to make sure Blake's camera is always ready. I don't even remember doing it, it's so automatic."

"You took the used film out of his camera and replaced it with a new roll."

"Yes. I always drop the exposed rolls into my camera bag, my knapsack. Always. It's second nature. Then the next day we develop them in the lab."

"Only this time you didn't do that."

"No. I didn't even realize I had the film. Billy's death, the police, the tabloids, I just…forgot." She felt like an idiot!

"The following week your purse was snatched, but not your camera bag?" He glanced at the now-empty green knapsack.

"No." Then it dawned on her why. "I almost always have it with me. Except I didn't the night I walked home from the police station. I'd left it at the precinct, just forgot it. An officer brought it by my apartment the next day."

"It doesn't look like a camera bag. Just an old knapsack, something you'd carry your lunch in. It wouldn't have been the thief's first target."

Her heart skipped a beat when she saw the exposed canister, recognized the speed designation that Blake preferred for indoor nighttime shots. "Here it is.'' She held it up to the firelight and they both looked at it.

''What's on it?''

''I don't know.'' But she could guess. Blake having sex with Billy. Only that, in and of itself, wasn't enough to warrant all that had happened since.

''Blackmail?'' Joe speculated.

''I don't think so. Blake doesn't have any money.''

''But his wife does.''

''True.''

''Barrett might have hired this guy himself to get the film back from you.''

She shook her head, uncomfortable with the idea. Not because she wouldn't put it past him, but because it didn't make sense. ''All he would have had to do is ask me for it. I would have given it to him, no questions asked. Besides, Blake doesn't know where I am.''

Joe looked at her. ''Well, whoever it is that wants it, has obviously already gotten to him.''

''Blake told this—'' she didn't like thinking about him ''—this creep, that I had it.''

''No, you don't,'' Joe said, and snatched the film from her hand. ''I have it.''

The door crashed open, startling them, spraying wood splinters across the room. Wendy's heart stopped. Joe dropped the film and went for his gun. Too late.

The man who'd attacked her that afternoon pointed an automatic weapon at her chest. ''Don't even think about it, Hero Boy.''

Chapter 12

Dressed in predator-gray camouflage and sporting what looked to Joe like a 9 mm seven-round Makarov, their uninvited guest wore a black ski mask over his face.

Which was significant.

That, coupled with the fact that he'd had dozens of opportunities to off them over the past week, but hadn't, told Joe he didn't intend to kill them now. If Wendy was right, all this guy wanted was the film.

"Who are you?" Joe said, careful not to move.

"You don't need to know that."

Wendy sat, frozen, next to him, her eyes wide with fear. "Wh-who sent you?"

"You definitely don't need to know that. You don't wanna know it." The man took another step into the cabin. Cold air blasted in behind him. Wendy shuddered.

"It's okay." Joe shot her what he hoped was a reassuring look.

"Yeah, peachy," the man said. "Okay, let's have it."

"Wh-what?" Wendy's voice quavered.

"Dumb, as well as blond, huh?" He nodded at the dozens of canisters littering the floor around them. "The film, bitch. Now."

With his eyes, Joe warned her not to move. "Come and get it," he said to the guy.

His gaze narrowed on Joe's weapon. "Nice piece. Take it out, why don't ya. Slide it over here, real slow."

Joe sized him up, guessing height, weight, noticing the set and color of his eyes, his pale skin tone, the brown scraggly hair sticking out from under the mask, committing to memory all the small details he'd need to later relate to the State Troopers. "You alone?" he said.

"Like I'd need any help to deal with you two?"

Joe breathed. All week he'd seen evidence of only one man tracking them, but had to be certain. Now he knew for sure Camo Man was alone.

Slowly he removed his forty-five from its holster, conscious of the fact that the bastard's gun was trained on Wendy. He might not want to kill her, but he could, Joe knew, if forced or if spooked. The thought of it made his mouth go dry. Sweat broke out on his forehead.

"Yeah, that's right. Nice and easy. Slide it across the floor to me." Joe had no choice. He did it. Camo Man knelt, retrieved it and jammed it into the pocket of his jacket. "Good decision."

Joe glared at him. "Okay. Take your film and go."

"No!" Wendy said.

Damn it! Now wasn't the time for her to be reckless or cavalier.

"No?" Camo Man took another step into the room.

He was so close now that, if Joe lunged, he could probably knock him off his feet. But it was too risky.

"What's the matter, babe? Got some nasty little pictures you don't want me to see?"

"I have no idea what you're talking about." Wendy drew herself up and tipped her chin at him. Joe warned her with his eyes a second time, but she ignored him. "This film is mine. Wildlife shots. Nothing you'd be interested in. Or, if you are, you can buy the magazine when it comes out next month."

He laughed and shot Joe a look. "She's good, isn't she? I like her. I'm gonna like her even more in a few minutes."

Damn it!

He moved his weapon into line with Joe's head.

"Don't!" Wendy said. "Here, take it. Take it all."

Joe felt a tightening in his chest as Wendy gathered up all the rolls and stuffed them into the green knapsack. All but one. An exposed roll she jammed purposely under his leg as she collected the others. He glimpsed the speed—four hundred—and knew it was the low-light indoor film Wendy had retrieved from Blake's camera.

"T-take it," she said, and offered him the knapsack.

"Bring it to me." His eyes gleamed in the firelight with what Joe instantly recognized as lust.

"No!" He grabbed her arm, pulled her back.

Camo Man stepped closer, swung his gun directly at Wendy's face. "Do it!"

"Okay, okay!" Despite Joe's protests, Wendy extracted herself from his grasp and stood.

"Over here." Camo Man waved her closer.

Joe's throat closed. His hands were clammy, his heart beating out of control. He had to do something. No way was that son of a bitch getting his hands on her.

"It's okay." Wendy looked at him, nodding, her expression calm. "It'll be okay." She walked toward the intruder, head high, her gaze locked on his. The guy outweighed her by at least a hundred pounds.

Christ, he had to do something *now.*

He still had his buck knife, sheathed in leather, hanging from his belt. Camo Man hadn't bothered relieving him of it. He'd never used it as a weapon, and didn't think he could free it before the guy shot him, but he'd have to take the chance if what he thought was coming next actually happened.

Wendy stopped a foot from him, cool as a cucumber, the 9 mm pointed directly at her chest.

Camo Man smiled, then did something Joe hadn't expected. He pulled his mask off. Joe stopped breathing. Wendy took a step back.

"Don't get any closer to him! Come back."

She shook her head, remembering, Joe knew, the incident that afternoon in the woods. Paralyzed, he watched, as the man nudged her breast with his gun. "Take 'em off."

"Wh-what?"

"Your clothes." He smiled, his eyes roving her body.

Joe felt rage coil inside him unlike anything he'd ever experienced.

"Okay," Wendy said, stunning him. "Just give me a minute." Her voice was controlled, even.

He'd seen her like this before—on the bridge a few days ago, crawling out onto the ledge that afternoon, and now, facing her attacker, a rapist and soon-to-be murderer, if Joe's intuition was correct.

Slowly Wendy turned her back to the man and unbuttoned her long-sleeved shirt. She met Joe's gaze, tried to convey something with her eyes that he wasn't certain he understood. Almost imperceptibly she nodded, then turned to face her attacker, slipping out of her shirt, her white satin bra shimmering orange in the firelight.

"Nice," Camo Man said.

Joe had to forcibly hold himself in check as Wendy stepped into the man's one-armed embrace. He couldn't imagine what she felt at that moment, and had never seen anything more courageous in his life.

The 9 mm wavered in Camo Man's hand, distracted by Wendy's apparent submission and his own mounting lust.

A heartbeat later, she made the move Joe knew was coming, and he was ready for it. Like a mad dog, he launched himself off the hardwood and went for the gun. Camo Man fired. Wendy screamed. The shot missed, and all three of them went down, hitting the floor.

His hand was on the gun, all his weight bearing down. A feral rage infused his blood, but Wendy was between them. Camo Man swore. Joe rolled left, wrenching the gun with him, and she slid free.

"Run!" he cried. "Get out!"

But she couldn't get out. They were blocking the door. Struggling for control of the weapon, they rolled again, Camo Man on top. The guy was huge, had weight and experience on him, but Joe knew he would win. He knew it. He would win because he had more to lose.

The gun went off between them, and Joe swore.

Wendy screamed his name.

Paralyzed, she stood over them for the longest seconds of her life, unable to speak or form a coherent thought. Her mind registered Joe's voice, saw his blood-covered arm slide limply out from under their attacker's prone form.

"Oh, God." She knelt, grabbed the man's jacket and tried to pull him off. "Stop it! Stop it!" He wouldn't move, was heavier than she'd expected. Panic closed her throat as her knee slid into something warm, blood pooling on the floor. "Get off him!"

He couldn't be dead! He just couldn't! Why couldn't she move the guy? Why wouldn't he get off? She jumped as the handgun clattered onto the floor.

"It's okay," Joe said softly. The breath rushed out of her as she heard his voice. With a grunt Joe pushed the man aside and was free of him.

Wendy was suddenly there, pulling him to her, her gaze fixed in horror on his blood-soaked shirt.

"It's not mine," he said, his hands going around her waist. "It's…his."

Her arms slid around his neck, and they tumbled backward in an awkward embrace. She said his name over and over, couldn't stop herself.

"It's okay," he reassured her. "I'm okay."

"He's...dead?" She glanced at the body lying next to them.

"Yeah."

"You're sure?"

"I'm sure, babe. He's dead."

That's why he hadn't moved when she'd touched him. That's why he'd felt so heavy. Dead weight, she thought, and now knew what the term really meant.

"Oh, Joe!" She closed her eyes and relived the moment when the gun had gone off the second time, felt again the panic that had seized her.

"You're safe now. I'm with you." He sat up with her in his arms, brushed the hair out of her face so he could see her. "You okay?"

She nodded, letting her breath go.

"Sure?"

Nodding again, she said, "Yes." As long as you're with me, she thought. As long as you don't leave me for a second.

"Come on. Let's get up." He got her to her knees, then helped her up.

She stared at the dead man at their feet. Now that it was over, she thought she would faint. Her knees buckled. Joe grabbed her around the waist and eased her onto one of the bunks.

"No, I'm okay," she said, suddenly chilled, aware of her bare midriff and white bra, her hands and face, all sticky with blood. Joe was covered in it. "We need to...clean up." Again she glanced at the man.

"I'll take care of him. You take care of yourself. The water's hot by now." He nodded at the potbelly stove, where the forgotten bucket of bathwater sat simmering.

"Okay."

He grabbed a tarp from the blue pack and some nylon cording, and in less than a minute had fashioned a drape across the back corner of the cabin. She watched him, still in shock over what had happened, as he poured the steaming water into the tub.

"Be right back," he said, stepping over the dead man's body with the bucket, heading for the open door.

She had to force herself to sit still, to nod, as if it was fine that he was leaving her alone for the minute it would take him to draw more water from the river. It wasn't okay. She didn't want him to leave her. Not now. Not ever.

To calm herself she focused on the bath. How good it would feel. She searched inside the blue pack for her liquid soap. Biodegradable, good for dishes, hair, clothes, bodies, everything. Her mind was babbling.

"Here we go." Joe poured a bucket of cold water into the tub and checked the temperature with his hand. "It's good. Go ahead. I'll uh—" he nodded at the body "—take him outside."

"Wh-who is he?"

"I don't know, but I'm gonna find out." He glanced at the dead man again, then looked at her.

She realized she was standing there in her bra, but she didn't care. His gaze washed over her in the firelight, and she let him look, the natural instinct to cover herself nonexistent.

"Wendy," he said, and stroked her cheek.

She wanted to rush into his arms, hold him, never let go, but didn't. "I'll just be a few minutes," she said, and glanced at the bathwater.

"Take your time."

She moved behind the drape and closed her eyes, breathing in, out, working to get ahold of herself. As she undressed, she heard the unmistakable sounds of Joe dragging the body outside.

When he returned, she was sitting on one of the bunks wrapped in nothing but a blanket. Her hair was damp, her face still pale, but her eyes were themselves again, calm, alert, as blue as any summer sky he'd ever seen.

"Where…is he?" she said.

"Don't worry about it."

He saw that she'd used soap and some of her bath-water to scrub the floor of the cabin where the fatal shot that had killed their attacker had been fired. A wet, blood-soaked T-shirt lay in the corner of the room. He didn't have the heart to tell her it was a crime scene, that she probably shouldn't have done it.

"I would have taken care of that," he said.

"It's okay. I'm fine. Really."

But she wasn't fine. He could see it in her expression, in the way she moved, slow and mechanically.

"Did you find out who he is?"

"Yeah." He pulled the guy's wallet out of his pocket and read the name off his driver's license. "Dwight Carson."

"Never heard of him," Wendy said.

He read a couple of phone numbers aloud that were scribbled on the back of a business card engraved with a name that Wendy said sounded familiar to her. One of the numbers had a New York area code, the other had a code he didn't recognize.

Wendy's eyes widened. "The first one's Blake's number. The second one is my parents' house in Michigan. Oh, God."

"He can't hurt you now. Or them." He looked at her sitting on the bunk, and she seemed so small, so vulnerable. He wanted to take her in his arms and tell her not to worry, that everything was going to be okay, that he was going to take care of it and take care of her.

She stared at the blood on his shirt, then nodded at the tub in the corner. "We…need more water."

He sucked in a breath and looked down at his clothes, his hands. He wanted to tend to her but needed to clean up first. Besides, she hadn't dressed—not that he necessarily wanted her to, but she would want to. He'd give her some time, a little privacy.

"I'll manage in the creek outside. There're a couple of deep pools."

"You'll freeze."

He knew she was naked under the blanket. He wondered what she'd do if he came over there, eased her back onto the bunk and kissed her. He wondered what she'd feel like with him inside her.

Get a grip, Peterson.

That's not what she needed now. That's not even what she wanted, not from him. She needed comfort, reassurance, not sex.

He also knew what he was feeling for her wasn't just sexual. And that scared the hell out of him.

"It'll do me good," he said, grabbing the soap and his makeshift shaving kit, shaking off the foreign feelings. "Here, keep this with you." He laid his forty-five, which he'd retrieved from Carson's pocket, beside her on the bunk. "Just in case."

Leaving her sitting there, he retreated outside and closed the door.

She waited for him, knowing what would happen when he returned. Wanting it to happen.

When the door finally opened, she tensed. He froze in the doorway, clean shaven, barefoot and bare-chested, his trousers slung low on his hips, his belt undone, his shirt balled up in his fist, dripping water.

"Oh," he said, noticing she was still sitting there wrapped in the blanket. "You need more time. I'll just—"

"No."

He stopped, looked at her, his gaze locking on hers like a cruise missile.

"I'm ready for you to come in. I'm...ready for you."

He didn't say anything, just closed the door behind him, locked it, all without taking his eyes off her. He tossed his wet shirt in the corner with hers.

Wendy opened the blanket.

As he walked toward her, knelt on the floor beside the bunk, put his hand on her knee, she knew there was no going back. She also knew he was all wrong for her. Stubborn, controlling, used to getting his own way and making every decision, shouldering every consequence alone.

But watching the firelight dance in his eyes as his gaze slid like silk over her bare skin, she didn't care. She just wanted him.

"You're sure?" His hand moved up her leg, the electricity of his touch causing her breath to catch.

"No," she whispered.

"That's okay." He climbed into the bunk on top of her, grazed a finger along her jaw, across her parted lips. "I am."

Chapter 13

Abandoning her fears, all her good sense, turning off the voice in her head telling her she was making a huge mistake, Wendy closed her eyes and kissed him.

He slid his arms beneath her, and her legs opened to receive him. Settling his weight on top of her, he deepened the kiss. His tongue was hot, but his skin was cool from the river, and the feel of his hard chest against her breasts forced her nipples to instantly harden.

He shuddered, and she gasped, fearing to open her eyes and look at him. She knew if she did, she'd be lost. He breathed her name between kisses, his hands sliding downward to cup her buttocks, his erection pressing into her through the coarse fabric of his pants.

When she felt his mouth on her breast, she cried out, throwing her head back, arching into him.

Groaning, he gripped her almost viciously, undulated against her, kissed her with a raw hunger that made her wild with need.

She responded, clawing at his back, his trousers, trying to work them off his hips. And then she made an uncalculated mistake. She opened her eyes, her gaze connecting with his, their lips a breath apart, and what she read in his face scared her.

"Wendy." He brushed her lips with his, looking at her with eyes she'd never seen before, dark and hooded, with more than lust reflecting back at her in the firelight.

He grasped her chin, made her look at him, whispered endearments meant to calm her frenzy, slow her mounting passion so he could connect with her, engage her emotions.

"Oh, Joe." She needed him, yes, wanted him desperately to take her mind away from the events of the past hour, the past month, to make her feel safe, to help her forget, if just for a little while, who she was and all that had happened.

Moments ago, sitting on the bunk waiting for him, she'd told herself it was just sex that she needed, a physical coupling, a release. That she could handle it, and that he could, too. But now, looking into his eyes, she knew it wasn't just sex, not for him. Not for her.

He kissed her, softly this time, rolling his hips gently into hers. "Wendy, I—"

She kissed him hard, her heart pounding, fearing the words she knew were poised on his lips. Her hand slid between his legs, and he responded, giving in to the physical, kissing, biting, groping her, pushing himself into her hand, his need intensifying.

She closed her eyes and lost herself in his touch, the feel of his bare chest against hers, the minty scent of his hair newly shampooed with her soap, dripping cool water on her heated skin.

He was rock hard and ready. So was she.

Together they eased his pants off. Seconds later he slid into her, both of them crying out with the shock of it, her legs wrapping tightly around his hips. No more thinking, no more fears. He thrust into her, over and over, giving himself up to her, and she to him, their eyes locked, their emotions laid bare.

When he slipped his hand between them, she thought she'd go mad.

He did when he watched her come apart.

The sound of the river took his mind away, along with the cold. Joe stretched out, naked, on a long flat slab of basalt outside the cabin and gazed at the clear night sky. A billion stars winked back at him from a field of midnight velvet.

He was so relaxed he didn't hear the cabin door open, or Wendy pad barefoot across a late-summer patch of wild grass to join him.

"Hey," she said, startling him.

He sat up and saw that she was wrapped in the down sleeping bag that they'd unzipped and had used as a blanket in the bunk.

"Aren't you cold?" She eased down next to him on the rock and offered him part of it.

Smiling, he pulled her down with him, then zipped the sleeping bag around them so they were warmly cocooned. Together they stared at the sky, his arm around her, her head tucked into the crook of his shoulder, her hand splayed across his chest, her fingers toying with his hairs.

He couldn't remember the last time he felt this good. Hell, maybe never.

By silent consent they didn't talk about Dwight Carson, or the fact that Joe had wrapped his body in a plastic tarp and stashed it in the narrow storage locker running along the outside of the DF&G cabin. It would have to stay there until he got Wendy out of the reserve and could call in the State Troopers to retrieve it.

The incident lay heavy on both their minds, but he knew for tonight they wouldn't speak of it. He'd push it from his thoughts until tomorrow, when the light of day would bring with it the reality of their situation.

He was in love with her, but she wasn't in love with him, or at least he didn't think she was.

Could he blame her? He couldn't even protect her. He'd let Carson get to her twice.

"Tell me about your boyfriends," he said, not really wanting to know about them, but wondering why a woman like her had never married. Never even been close, he remembered her saying.

She took a breath, exhaled with a little sigh. "There's not much to tell, really. I've had a few, but none were really serious. Well, they never got the chance to be."

"Why not?" He looked at her, and she shrugged in his arms.

"I was always working too much."

"By choice?"

"Not really. Blake was a bit of a slave driver,

especially where I was concerned. He said I had to pay my dues.''

''And I'll bet those dues were steeper when there was a man in your life.''

''You're right, they were.'' She rolled onto her back and looked at the sky. ''Blake was jealous. Every time I started dating somebody new, he'd become impossible to work with.''

''He wanted you for himself.'' Joe couldn't wait to get his hands on this guy.

''He did. Only, I didn't know that when I first took the job out of college. It never even crossed my mind. He was married.''

''Doesn't sound like that meant much to him.''

''No, it didn't. He was always having affairs— with women, I mean. I hadn't known about…well, you know.''

Joe didn't want to think about it.

''Blake always found a way to sabotage my relationships. I can see now that he was punishing me for refusing to sleep with him.''

''Why did you stay? There had to have been other jobs you could have taken.''

''There were. Lots of them in the beginning. But Blake was the best and kept telling me how lucky I was to be working for him, to have him as a mentor.''

''Some mentor.''

''I know.'' She rolled into his arms. ''I was stupid. I believed I wasn't good enough, that I was nothing without him. But that part of my life is over. I'm different, smarter. No one's ever going to manipulate or control me like that again.''

He held her, nuzzling her hair, brushing kisses

across her temple. The cut she'd sustained during the rock slide was still visible, a thin red line. The more he thought about Barrett and this guy Carson, the angrier he got.

"You gave him the caribou film."

"Hmm?"

Joe hadn't wanted to talk about it, but needed to know. "When you gathered up the film to give to Carson, you saved the exposed roll from the loft, but were going to give him your magazine shots."

"I had to. I figured I could sneak one roll past him if I was quick. I don't know what's on that film, but I suspect it's something more than just one of Blake's flings. Besides, that…creep was going to kill you."

Now, when he thought back on it, he knew Carson would have done exactly that. "You would have let him…hurt you." The thought of her allowing Carson to rape her to protect him was more than he could take.

"To save your life?" She looked at him in the starlight with wide silvery eyes. "I would have, but I knew I wouldn't have to. I knew that, together, we'd be able to stop him."

Together.

Now that was a new concept for him, one he knew he wasn't comfortable with. He'd fully expected he would stop Carson on his own. He'd never even considered that Wendy might be able to help. But that's exactly what she'd done. In fact, if she hadn't distracted Carson, he would never have been able to subdue him without one of them getting hurt or killed.

He closed his eyes and tried to forget the fear he'd

felt when she'd walked into Carson's arms. "Come here," he said, and rolled her on top of him. She was warm and soft and sleepy, and he never wanted to let her go.

"Make me forget." She kissed him, rolling her hips seductively into his groin, making him instantly hard. "Make me forget everything."

He did, sliding her down onto his shaft, suckling her breasts as she began to move in a rhythm that made his blood burn through his veins, that caused the sky to spin above their heads at warp speed.

She threw her head back, grinding into him, and a burst of color shimmered on the horizon, an eerie green he saw reflected in her eyes.

"Northern lights," she whispered, seeing them, too, then gave herself up to the rising wave of pleasure neither of them could hold back, even if they'd wanted to.

Holding her hips in place, he thrust harder, flashing on the fact that they hadn't used a condom either time. He wondered if she'd get pregnant. The thought of it made him wild, like an animal.

He drove himself inside her.

The next morning the reality of their situation settled into her bones like the icy fog blanketing the valley for the second day in a row. Wendy shuddered as Joe secured the cabin and checked, for the dozenth time, the padlock on the outside storage locker.

"He's in there," she said, knowing all along that's where Joe had put the body. It was the only suitable place, protected from animals and from discovery by other hikers—not that there *were* any other hikers.

"It's cold enough that…well, you know."

So that the body would keep until the State Troopers arrived. A chill wriggled up her spine.

"Cold?" He put an arm around her shoulder.

"No, just…anxious. We should get a move on."

"Yeah. It's sixty-two miles to the station from here. Four days if we move fast."

"Three if we hike dawn-to-dusk." They were both in good shape, and the trail was nearly all downhill from here on out.

As he guided her onto the path, she glanced back at the cabin where she'd spent both the worst and the best night of her life.

A man was dead because of a roll of film, and the man who'd killed him and who walked beside her now was both everything she wanted and everything she feared.

"There was something I wanted to say last night but didn't."

She heard him, but kept walking, moving out from under his arm, ahead of him onto the trail. She wasn't ready for this. Or maybe she was, and that's what scared her the most.

"Thanks," he said, surprising her.

She turned to look at him, thinking how foolish she was. She'd thought he was going to tell her that he— Oh, hell. "For what?"

"For what you did last night."

She thought of their lovemaking, and how that second time she'd been a bit bold, but knew from the gravity of his expression that wasn't what he meant.

"With Carson. What you did took guts. I just wanted to say thanks."

She smiled at him. "It was a team effort, if I remember correctly."

"Yeah," he said, not returning her smile. "A team."

They walked in silence the rest of the morning, each absorbed in their own thoughts, conscious of each other in the way that only new lovers are. Except, for her it was different.

She'd never felt like this before, and for that reason she kept her pace brisk, avoiding letting him follow too closely behind her. A couple of times while they were walking, he touched her, toyed with her hair, and she had to stop herself from turning and going into his arms.

The farther they got from the cabin, the more she resisted him emotionally, steeling herself for the moment they'd reach the station and she'd be connected again to the world she was going back to and was intent on making a life in.

She reminded herself that Joe Peterson was out here in the middle of nowhere for a reason. He'd narrowed his own world into one he could control, or one he thought he could. She didn't have to remind herself that he was all wrong for her. He did that himself at every turn, his take-charge attitude escalating in direct proportion to her emotional distance.

They stopped rarely, only to discuss the trail or the fog, which hung on like a long winter. The river was with them the whole way, its rushing waters drowning out all other sounds. At a blind turn in the trail, Joe stepped in front of her, making it clear he was going first.

She knew what had happened with Carson last night had scared the hell out of him. Her, too. They'd almost gotten killed. He was just being extra careful today. Still, the brusque way he'd sidestepped her, without so much as an explanation, irritated her.

He charged around the corner, one hand absently resting on his holstered gun. Wendy was right behind him, her dander up. Seconds later they got the shock of their lives.

"Jesus!" Joe pulled up short.

They'd been moving so fast she lost her footing trying not to run into him from behind. The next thing she knew she was facedown in the dirt, sprawled at his feet.

"Doctor Livingstone, I presume!"

Wendy looked up to see Barb Maguire's beaming smile fixed on Joe, her black springy curls twisted to Shirley Temple proportions in the fog.

A big, beefy guy with bright-blue eyes and an identical smile stood beside her, a gargantuan pack on his back. Before Wendy could react, he offered her a paw the size of a small ham. "And, uh, Mrs. Livingstone?"

Wendy grabbed his hand at the same time Joe took hold of her upper arm, and together the two men hauled her to her feet. She was still wiping the mud off her clothes when introductions were made.

"This is the old ball and chain," Barb said.

"Stan Maguire." The big man offered her his hand again. "Wendy, right?"

She nodded, watching, as Barb instantly appraised the situation, noticing the way Joe's arm had absently slipped around her shoulder, pulling her close as Stan shook her hand.

Barb's grin broadened. "Well, looks like you two are okay, after all."

"What are you doing here?" Joe abruptly removed his arm.

"Four days ago," Stan said, "I was tagging some fish in 34A and spotted a car up one of those spur roads east of the reserve."

Wendy remembered that Barb's husband was a Department of Fish and Game biologist.

Stan's smile vanished, his face all business now. "Turns out it was stolen. Troopers checked it out and found this." He retrieved a familiar-looking luggage tag from his pants pocket and handed it to her.

"It's mine!" Wendy turned the tag over in her hand, reading her name and her parents' Michigan address.

"Yeah, and when they jimmied the trunk they found all your gear."

"Carson," Joe said.

"Who?" Barb frowned.

"Anyway, we were worried. Saw your truck and her SUV at the end of the east road and decided to come in after you."

"You got to the pass?"

Stan nodded. "Saw what had happened, found your pack on top. Got it in the back of my truck."

"Thanks, man."

Barb shot him a look. "After they found Wendy's luggage, I begged the boss to get the DF&G chopper outta Spalding, but nooo." Wendy had seen Spalding on the map. It was a bigger town, about two hundred miles away.

"Chief wouldn't go for it," Stan said. "Didn't wanna spend the money. Troopers wouldn't send one, either, till we were sure something was really wrong."

"Well, there is, and we're going to need one."
Joe quickly related the events of the past week.
Barb's brown eyes widened, and when he told them
what had happened in the cabin last night, her mouth
dropped open.

"Son of a salmon!" Stan ran a beefy hand over
his face, then looked at Wendy, more keenly this
time, concern shining in his eyes. "You okay?"

She nodded. "Lucky for me, Joe was with me."
She met his gaze, remembering both yesterday's terrible events and its tender ones.

"Geez," Barb said, not missing a thing. "I'm glad
I told you she was in here."

It was clear from Joe's quick change of expression
that he was still angry at Barb for issuing her a wilderness permit. Warden Rambo didn't easily forgive.
"Let's get out of here," he said, and, not gently, took
her arm.

"Maybe Barb and I should go on to the cabin and…
you know, secure the crime scene. For this kinda
thing, Troopers'll call in SCIB from Fairbanks."

"SCIB?"

"The Statewide Criminal Investigations Bureau,"
Joe explained.

Wendy watched Stan's face as he did the math in
his head. "Could be five, six days."

"Don't bother," Joe said. "Everything's secure,
and there's no one in the reserve except us."

The two men conferred for a few minutes, Joe re-
lating more details about Dwight Carson's actions
over the past week, and what had happened in the
cabin last night.

"You knew this guy?" Stan asked her.

"No."

Joe nodded toward the trail. "I'll fill you in while we walk. Come on," he said, and guided her onto the path. "Fog's lifting."

The weather cooperated, and after three and a half days of hard, fast hiking, the foursome reached Joe's station. Wendy was never so glad to see a place in her life. They were all exhausted. Barb had blisters, Stan looked as if he was ready to collapse, and Joe hadn't said a word to any of them for the past four miles.

They'd spent two nights together in DF&G cabins, and one in the rough, their tents pitched side by side. Wendy and Joe hadn't had any privacy in days, which was probably for the best, she thought, as she watched him climb the last few feet up the hill to the station.

His face was grim, his eyes cool and eagle sharp, reminding her of the day she met him, nearly two weeks ago. Joe Peterson was back in his realm and fully in charge, all business and heightened control.

They hadn't made love since the night Carson had attacked them in the cabin, though Joe had held her each night as she slept, bone tired, and kissed her when she'd allowed it.

They'd both been holding themselves in check. She knew their cautious behavior wasn't because they were shy around Stan and Barb. The couple had given them numerous opportunities to be alone, but neither she nor Joe had acted on them. It was almost as if their one night together had been a fantasy, as if she'd only imagined it. And now, four short days later, reality was back.

"My truck!" Joe walked toward the green pickup parked beside what she guessed was Stan's four-wheel-drive.

"Figured you'd want it." Stan fished a set of keys out of his pocket and tossed them to him. "I had Barb drive it back from the trailhead." He turned to Wendy. "We had to leave your SUV. Joe can take you to get it later."

"That's fine. I don't think I'll be heading back to New York until tomorrow."

Joe shot her a look she couldn't decipher.

Barb evidently could, because the normally cheery woman who'd become her friend over the past few days arched dark brows at her in an "uh-oh" sort of way.

It was only midday, but Wendy was drained, both physically and emotionally. She had half a dozen phone calls to make, and return travel arrangements to New York to confirm.

She knew both she and Joe would have to go into town to make formal statements to the authorities about Dwight Carson's death. Joe had assured her it would be written off as a clear case of self-defense.

They tromped up the stairs and into the station, packs and all, shucked their gear and outerwear and collapsed in Joe's front room. All except Joe. He slid a hip onto his office desk and grabbed the phone. A minute later he was talking to the Statewide Criminal Investigations Bureau of the Alaska State Troopers.

Wendy closed her eyes and sank deeper into the sofa, listening, as Joe described the situation over the phone. "*C-a-r-s-o-n.* Dwight Carson. Right. New York driver's license number…"

She tuned out, not wanting to remember.

"Yeah," Joe said, winding down the call. "We'll come on in this afternoon." When he hung up the phone, he looked at her. "SCIB wants to talk you— about something else."

"What?"

"I don't know. They wouldn't say."

Barb mumbled something about making coffee, and disappeared into the kitchen. Stan got the hint and followed her. When Joe walked over to the sofa and sat down beside her, Wendy fought the urge to reach for him.

"You okay?"

She nodded, taking in her filthy clothes, the dirt caked under her broken nails and the assorted bruises and scratches she'd sustained over the past ten days. "I could use an hour-long shower and a steak."

"You got it." He squeezed her knee reassuringly, then looked at her with a question in his eyes she wasn't ready to answer.

"I have to go back," she said.

"Not right away, you don't."

"I do. I've got to get this cleared up. I need to call Blake. We need to know what's on that film."

Joe reached into his pocket and produced the exposed film canister, which he hadn't given back to her since the incident in the cabin. "It's evidence. I'm turning it over to SCIB."

"Evidence of what?" She snatched it from his hand. "Before we do anything, before *I* do anything, I have to know what I'm involved in."

She watched him as he considered her point. For the first time his unrelenting need to control things worked in her favor. Finally he said, "Barb's nephew has an amateur darkroom in town. Borough cops and state troopers use it when they're short on time and don't want to send stuff to the SCIB lab in Fairbanks. For something this important, though, we ought to have a pro develop it.''

''I *am* a pro.''

His gaze raked her over appreciatively. ''A damned good one, too.''

Last night she'd overheard him telling Stan about the caribou photos. Pride had bubbled up inside her like a root beer float, tickling her stomach, when she'd caught the animation in Joe's eyes and the excitement in his voice as he related the story.

''Let's do it, then,'' she said, and pocketed the film.

''This afternoon. Right now you're going to have that shower, and I'll rustle us up some steaks.''

''Oh, man, don't tempt me.'' Stan lumbered in from the kitchen, his eyes lighting up at the sound of food.

''Tempt you with what?'' Barb breezed past him like a seasoned Octoberfest waitress, bearing four full mugs of coffee.

''Steaks. But we gotta go.'' Stan took one of the mugs from her and downed it in a couple of swallows. ''Gotta get back to town. The boss is gonna have a cow when he hears about this.''

''He's next on my list to call.'' Joe started for the kitchen, and by the time he returned a minute later with a to-go cup for Barb's coffee, Stan was already maneuvering his wife out the door.

''Take care, buddy.'' Stan clapped him on the shoulder. ''You don't know if this Carson guy has friends.''

Wendy suspected he did, though they hadn't seen

signs of any accomplices, at least not here in Alaska. As much as she didn't want to, she knew she had to call Blake. Later, she'd contact the detective in New York who'd investigated Billy Ehrenberg's death, but first she had to know what was going on, and she had to know now.

"How about that shower," Joe said, waving good-bye to the Maguires and steering her toward the bathroom.

Her mind leaped into overdrive, considering again all the possibilities of what had really happened that night in the loft. She crashed back to the moment when Joe handed her a stack of towels. "Um, sounds good."

"Want me to scrub your back?" He nuzzled her ear, and she made herself back away, out of his arms.

"N-no. I, uh, think I need some time alone."

Right now she couldn't think about what had happened between them, what *was* between them. She couldn't even think about the magazine or her caribou photos. Until she got this thing with Blake and Billy and the film cleared up, she wouldn't be able to make any rational decisions about anything else in her life.

The look in Joe's eyes told her he was disappointed, but that he understood.

"Thanks," she said, and closed the bathroom door, shutting him out.

A half hour later, feeling like a new woman, clean and wrapped in a towel, her teeth sparkling, she emerged from the steam-filled bathroom. Joe was in the hall waiting for her. The smell of steaks sizzling on the outdoor grill made her mouth water.

"Better?"

"Much."

He opened his arms, and this time she didn't hesitate. She felt needy and unsure, and his warm embrace was like a tonic. His lips sought hers, and she gave in to his kiss, which was hot and desperate.

She knew he wanted to make love to her. She wanted it, too, but not now, not yet. She was confused, afraid—not only of what she felt for him, but of how everything that had happened in New York, and here, would play out. There were still too many unknowns, the most unnerving one looking at her now with hooded hazel eyes.

"I need a shower," he said. "Bad."

"Take a cold one."

He laughed, and she laughed with him. It was the first time in days they'd found anything to laugh about. It felt good, and reminded her that, once all of this was over, she would have a life again. Her life, whatever she chose to make of it.

"Be right back," he said, and brushed a kiss across her forehead. "Watch the steaks."

She forgot about the steaks and watched him as he stripped off his clothes and stepped into the shower. As if they were a couple, he hadn't even bothered to shut the bathroom door. The sight of his hard, muscular body and his half-aroused state almost made her change her mind and follow him in.

But she didn't. She waited until he'd pulled the curtain and had turned on the water before padding barefoot back into the front room.

It was late afternoon in New York. Securing the towel around her torso, she picked up the phone, dialed the number she knew by heart. No answer. On a hunch, she dialed another number, and her stomach balled in a knot when the phone on the other end of the line began to ring.

"H-hello."

Wendy almost didn't recognize the frail voice. "Vivian?" Blake's wife typically had no idea where her husband was, but it was worth a try. "Vivian, it's Wendy."

"Wendy. Oh, God."

"What is it, Viv? Where's Blake? Is he there? I really need to speak to him."

"You don't know?"

"Know what?"

Joe appeared in the doorway, naked and dripping wet, wrapping a towel around his hips. The shower was still running. "We're out of sham—" The look on her face stopped him.

She dragged her attention back to the call. Vivian was stumbling over her words. "Wait, Viv. Slow down. Where's Blake?"

Joe moved to her side, his eyes cool and questioning.

Vivian's words registered.

"Oh, my God."

"Wendy, what is it?" He gripped her arm, aware a split second before she was that her knees had given out beneath her.

"It's Blake." She dropped the phone, and Joe caught her in his arms. "H-he's dead."

Chapter 14

"Start over." Joe eased Wendy onto the sofa.

She realized she was shivering, and was grateful he'd wrapped her in the flannel bathrobe he'd retrieved from his bedroom. It smelled like him, and she burrowed into it, pulling her bare feet up under her onto the sofa.

"Tell me everything she said." Joe sat beside her, his arm sliding naturally around her shoulders, pulling her close. Wendy didn't resist.

"Sh-she said Blake had been missing for a-almost three weeks."

"And this Vivian, his wife, she was worried."

Wendy shook her head. "N-no. He went off all the time without telling her where he was going."

"Nice guy."

She didn't refute his sarcasm.

"Here, drink some of this. You'll feel better." He held a steaming coffee cup to her lips. He'd refilled both hers and his with more of the brew Barb had made earlier.

"Thanks," she said, and sipped at it, warming her hands on the cup.

"Then what?"

"Then the police showed up. Yesterday, if I understood her correctly. She was rambling out of control. Evidently, they'd found Blake's body in the woods about a mile from the house. Their house," she explained, "up in Connecticut. Blake kept an apartment in the city, but Vivian and the kids..."

She couldn't bear to think about his children. She could never forgive Blake for getting her involved in this mess, but she didn't wish him dead, either.

"He was murdered," Joe said.

The thought of it made her stomach clench. "Vivian said the police thought it was an accident. That he'd been out hiking and—"

"You said Barrett wasn't the hiking type."

"He's not." She looked at him. "I mean he... wasn't." She'd begun to think of Blake in the past tense weeks ago, but only because she'd put him out of her life, not because he was dead. The irony of it chilled her.

"I'm sorry he's dead."

"You are?" This was the first time Joe had ever expressed anything other than contempt for her former mentor.

"Damned right, I am. I was looking forward to having a little talk with the son of a bitch about what the hell he thought he was doing involving you in this."

"Oh." She set the coffee cup down. "And how, exactly, were you intending to do that? By phone?"

"No. I was thinking of going back to New York with you, to get all this settled."

She started to argue with him.

"It doesn't matter," he said over her protests. "All we have now is the film."

She got off a few more choice quips, and then it dawned on her. "What did you say?"

"I said, all we have is the film."

Wendy shot to her feet, the memory striking her like lightning. "No! We have more than that. The letter! We have Blake's letter!"

"Wait a minute." He followed her to the phone, where she was already punching in the number to her parents' house. "You said you threw it away."

"I did but—" She finished, waited for the call to connect. "Quick, what day is this?" She knew it was the fourteenth of August. Her photos were due to the magazine on the twenty-first, and she'd been keeping track of the date. "What day of the week, I mean?"

"I don't know, Wednesday." He glanced at the desk calendar to make sure.

"Mom?" She tried to remember when her parents' recycling went out. She knew it was picked up twice a month.

"Wendy? Wendy, we've been so worried! The police called here for you and—"

"Mom, not now. I need a favor."

"Wendy, what's this about?" Joe put his ear to the phone with hers so he could hear their conversation.

"And this horrible man came here looking for you the morning you left. He was big and had these dark eyes and—"

"Carson," Joe whispered.

"Mom, not now. I need you to do something for me." She explained that she'd tossed Blake's unread letter in their recycling bin. She begged her mother to go look for it.

While they waited, Joe said, "Do they have a fax machine?"

"No, but there's one in town at the local photocopy shop. She can fax it to us from there."

Her mother came back on the line. "It was crumpled into a little ball, but yes, I think this is it. Wendy?"

As patiently as her racing heart would allow, she instructed her mother to drive into town and fax them the letter.

"Well, okay, but I still wish you would tell me—" Her mother was abruptly cut off.

"Wendy?" At once she recognized the booming baritone of her father's voice, and he didn't sound happy.

"It's Dad," she said to Joe, covering the mouthpiece.

"Here, let me talk to him." Before she could stop him, Joe wrenched the receiver from her hand.

She spent the next five minutes glaring at him as he engaged in the kind of man-to-man conversation that men like Joe and her father relished. Only, the conversation was all about her, and it ended with Joe assuring her father that he would take care of her, that he would take care of everything.

"Happy now?" she said, folding her arms across her chest as he replaced the handset.

"Yeah. They're driving into town now. We should have the fax in about twenty minutes."

She didn't know whether to hug him or smack

him. The man was simply incapable of letting her deal with anything on her own. She realized that part of the problem was hers. She was overreacting, and had been ever since she'd met him. She was so intent on never letting anyone run her life again, she went off like a rocket each time he tried to help her.

"Jesus," Joe said, and glanced out the window at the smoke spewing from the barbecue.

She wrinkled her nose at the smell of burning steaks. "Sorry. I guess I forgot about them."

Joe's stomach audibly growled. "That's okay. I've got more in the freezer." He pulled her to him and kissed her. She let him, inhaling the clean warm scent of his skin. "Why don't you get dressed. There're some extra clothes of Cat's in the spare room. We can do your laundry tonight."

"Thanks." She glanced at the towel still wrapped around his hips and thought fleetingly of what was under it. "You should put something on, too. You'll catch cold."

He watched her as she left the room, the heat in his eyes making it clear to her that the notion wasn't very likely.

Just as they were diving in to a repeat performance of grilled steaks, the fax machine hummed to life. Wendy jumped up from the kitchen table so fast she knocked over her glass of milk.

"Leave it," Joe said, and followed her into the front room.

They watched as the pages appeared. Joe had to physically stop himself from ripping them off the machine. This was *her* letter, he reminded himself, and she'd made it clear that the nightmare she was involved in was her problem, not his, no matter how badly he wanted to solve it for her.

She'd shot him nasty looks the entire time he was on the phone with her father. Okay, so he might have overstepped his bounds a little, but he cared about her, damn it. What was wrong with that?

He loved her. He knew that now beyond a doubt, and it was tearing him up inside. He also knew if he told her, she'd bolt like a frightened deer. Hell, she was going to, anyway. Tomorrow, if she had her way.

"Here it is." Wendy snatched the pages off the machine and walked blindly to the sofa, her gaze riveted to the print.

Together, they sank into the cushions and, to Joe's surprise, she placed the letter in his lap. "I...can't," she said. "His handwriting looks so shaky. Will you read it to me?"

"Sure." He liked it that she asked him. She snaked her arm through his and snuggled close, and he liked that even more.

"Okay, here goes. *Willa*," he began, and stopped, rattled by the use of her pseudonym. She wasn't Willa, she was Wendy. *His* Wendy.

He glanced at the petite woman next to him who was fighting the urge to cling to him, and wondered what her life had been like in New York. He knew it was nothing like what he'd first envisioned. His year-long fixation on Cat's death, the fast lifestyle he knew his sister had led, all of that had colored his early impressions of Wendy, but no more.

In the past eleven days she'd demonstrated nothing but good sense, determination and moxie. The determination was sometimes overkill, but he admired that. Maybe she hadn't come into her own until recently, but she was there now. She was her own woman, a good woman.

A woman he wanted in his life.

Focusing his attention back on the letter, he was struck by the lack of a salutation, polite or otherwise. There was no *Dear Willa,* just *Willa.* "You have to know how sorry I am about—"

"Skip that part. I don't want to hear his apologies."

He scanned the next ten or twelve lines, then had to go to the second page. "Okay, here we go."

He read it to her slowly, stumbling over some of the hastily scrawled longhand. She was right. It looked as if Barrett was shaking like a leaf when he wrote it. Glancing back at the first page, he noted the date. Just ten days before Wendy had flown from her parents' house in Michigan to Alaska. He wondered how long it was after Barrett had written the letter that he'd ended up dead.

Not long, he suspected, given what was revealed in it. Barrett might have been a great photographer, but he hadn't been a very good businessman. He'd dug himself a hole trying to finance an expansion of his business. Vivian's parents had evidently cut him off from dipping further into her inheritance, and the banks wouldn't touch him, so he was forced to borrow an enormous amount of money from a loan shark. "A mob loan shark," Joe read.

"Oh, my God." Wendy ran her finger over the writing. "I had no idea."

The letter explained how Barrett had gotten himself into a jam and couldn't pay back the loan. To show good faith, that he was "willing to work with them,'' Barrett had agreed to set up a clandestine video session with Billy Ehrenberg, to be sold to a "private collector," one of the mob's clients.

Wendy looked at him. "I don't even want to think about what that means."

Joe didn't want to, either, but kept reading:

"Billy wasn't supposed to know he was being taped. When these thugs showed up and he found out, he went crazy. I'd set up my own camera thinking it would be fun to have some pictures for myself. I swear to God, Willa, if I'd known what was going to happen, I would have never—"

"Stop," Wendy said. "Don't read any more." She closed her eyes and rubbed her temples.

Joe scanned the remaining page of the letter. "There's nothing here. No mention of what happened next, no mention of the drugs. Nothing, except...

"You've got to return that film. At first I didn't realize you had it. All this time I thought *they* had it, but they don't. What's on that film implicates them, don't you see? I know you have it. They know you have it. These men mean business, Willa."

"That's for sure," she said, and pulled away from him.

Joe folded the faxed pages and stuffed them into the breast pocket of his shirt. He could guess what was captured on the film from Barrett's camera, in sequential, time-delayed shots.

Billy Ehrenberg's murder.

"Forget the darkroom idea. We have to turn the film over to law enforcement. Now."

"I know." She rose stiffly from the sofa. "Let's get it over with."

"Want to finish your steak before we go?"

"No, I've lost my appetite." Her face was pale, her movements sluggish.

Joe knew that the physical exertion of the past ten days, coupled with the emotional strain of Carson's attack, Barrett's letter, the film and their rapidly developing relationship was way too much for her to handle all at once. Hell, it was almost too much for him.

"We'll get something later in town, then." Gently he took her arm and led her to the door, grabbing their jackets and his truck keys on the way out.

Wendy felt numb during the two-and-a-half-hour ride into the town of Retreat.

She and Joe made small talk, carefully avoiding the topic that was the reason behind their trip. Wendy made him tell her about his college days and his early years with the Department of Fish and Game. She grilled him about his favorite foods, where he'd traveled, the kinds of movies and books he liked—anything to keep her mind occupied.

Joe settled easily into the exchange of their histories. He asked her about life in New York, what she'd done before moving there, to describe to him what it was like growing up in Michigan's north woods.

It was amazing how much they had in common. But then, she'd already known that. You learn a lot about a person spending every day and every night with them, as they had for the past week and a half.

She felt better by the time they reached town. She realized it was the first time they'd had a conversation that wasn't incited by a life-threatening situation or some flawed notion about the other's motives. It was just a normal conversation between two people who were interested in each other. She liked it.

He liked it, too, if she was reading him right. For the first time since they'd made love four days ago, he'd completely let down his guard with her. He wasn't trying to manage her, or the situation. He was relaxed, and so was she. Too bad it had to end.

He steered his pickup off the highway onto the gravel street that was the sleepy center of the town of Retreat. She'd stopped here on her way into the wildlife reserve and remembered the general store and gas pump on the corner, the funky-looking café down the street and the complex of newish buildings crafted of native stone.

They housed the post office, the state Department of Fish and Game—where she suspected Barb and Stan worked—and a small outpost of the Alaska State Troopers, which she'd learned had jurisdiction in areas like Retreat that were too small to support a police department.

"I'd like to show you something before we go in."

"What?" she asked, as he continued down the street and out of town.

"You'll see."

They passed a small graveyard, and she wondered

if Joe's sister was buried there. He didn't give it a glance as he proceeded up a hill into a small, heavily wooded residential area. When he turned onto a tiny dirt road, she was surprised to see it had a hand-carved street sign. Elkhorn Drive.

"Where are we going?"

"To my house."

"Your *house?*"

He shot her a smile. "Yeah. I built it before Cat died. Finished it but never moved in."

Her breath caught as he pulled into the driveway of a dramatic-looking log home, the kind you saw in magazines and dreamed about owning. It was two-story with a stone foundation and fireplace, and a rough-shingled, high-pitched roof. "It's gorgeous. You had this built?"

"I didn't have it built, I built it."

She got out of the truck, and by the time she finished gawking at the thick hand-hewn beams supporting the covered porch, he had the front door open.

"It's cold inside. The heat's off, but the electricity should be on. I haven't been here in a long time."

"You built it, you mean, like…with your hands?" Wendy had never seen more beautiful woodwork.

"Well," he said, grinning and taking her hand as they crossed the threshold, "I used power tools, of course. I'm not into the Amish thing, no matter how reclusive you think I am. And I had a hell of a lot of help. Stan mostly, and some of the other guys from town."

The interior was done all in warm woods, the rooms large and airy. Roughly shaved logs spanned the high, beamed ceilings.

She opened a door into what she thought was a bathroom. "Oh, is this for storage?"

"Yeah, I guess. It's the space under the staircase. Huge, isn't it? I'm not sure what to do with it. It's almost too big for a closet."

As Wendy stepped into the long, narrow room and switched on the overhead light, the hairs on the back of her neck prickled. "It's perfect," she said.

"For what? It's not like a real room, there're no windows."

"That's why it's perfect. For a darkroom!" She pictured it in her mind's eye. She'd never had her own darkroom, but had always wanted one, ever since she was a teenager.

"I never thought of that." He moved up beside her and put an arm around her shoulder, drawing her close.

She felt his body heat, his soft kiss just under her ear, and turned into him. "I didn't mean that—"

"I never had a reason to think of it, till now." He kissed her, and she melted into him.

His tongue was hot, his hands overbold as he backed her against the wall and deepened the kiss.

"Joe," she breathed against his lips, trying to extract herself from his embrace. He kissed her again, and she felt just how hot he was when he rolled his hips into hers. "Don't you think..." She kissed him back, her own heat building. "The State Troopers... shouldn't we..."

His hands moved to her breasts and she moaned, a heartbeat away from giving in to her own spiraling desire. "No," she said, and pressed firmly against his chest.

He backed off.

"I need to see the authorities. So do you. And then, tomorrow, I have to go back."

She meant back to New York. It never occurred to her to say back home, because the log house they were standing in, hand-built by the man who was looking at her with more than desire in his eyes, felt like home to her.

"Come on," she said, fighting her emotions. "Let's go."

Two four-wheel-drive State Trooper vehicles, Stan's truck and a nondescript sedan with government plates crowded the gravel parking lot of the cluster of buildings housing the Alaska State Trooper's outpost, the post office and the Department of Fish and Game. Joe pulled his truck in beside them, and they got out.

"Ready for this?" he said, and took her hand.

"No, but I want it over with."

"The sergeant you're going to talk to is a friend of mine, a real nice guy. There's nothing to worry about. Just tell him the truth."

"Thanks, Joe, for being with me through this. I know it hasn't been easy for you. I know *I* haven't been easy."

From the moment they'd met, she'd been sending him mixed signals. She'd done it again a few minutes ago in the log house on Elkhorn Drive. She wanted him, needed him, in fact, but *didn't* want to want or need him. The whole thing was crazy.

"I'm just…a little confused right now. I need to get on my feet, sort everything out in my mind."

He squeezed her hand, then let go. "I know. And I'm right here if you need me. And if you don't, I'll

try not to make you too mad by helping you, anyway.''

She couldn't help smiling. ''Thanks.''

''No problem.'' He opened the door for her, and
they went inside.

Chapter 15

Late in the day, after giving their statements and turning over the faxed letter and the film, Wendy and Joe emerged from the building that housed the small outpost of the Alaska State Troopers.

They'd each been interviewed separately by Joe's friend, the local sergeant. They'd also been questioned by an investigator from the Troopers' Statewide Criminal Investigations Bureau—SCIB—and an FBI agent, teleconferencing with the New York City police detective who'd handled the investigation into Billy Ehrenberg's and, as it turned out, Blake's deaths.

The interrogation had gone more smoothly than Wendy had expected. A helicopter shuttling the coroner and a crime scene unit out of Fairbanks was already on its way into the wildlife reserve to verify Joe's and Wendy's stories and to retrieve Dwight Carson's body.

The New York detective had told her the autopsy report on Blake had been finalized and that his death had been ruled a homicide. Carson was implicated. A hired hit man with a rap sheet a mile long and with ties to the mob, Dwight Carson had allegedly murdered Blake before following her to Michigan and, ultimately, Alaska.

His fingerprints had been subsequently found in her apartment, on her handbag and all over the luggage that had just been returned to her and that Joe was now lifting into the back of his truck.

"What now?" she said, slumping against the pickup.

He enfolded her in his arms, and she instantly felt better. "It's after six. How about something to eat. The café down the street makes a wicked moose burger."

"Sounds delicious," she deadpanned.

"Trust me, you'll love it."

Now that the worst was over, she was starved.

"Besides, the film's being developed as we speak. Barb left an hour ago with another Federal agent."

"They went to her nephew's darkroom?"

"Yeah. They should be back soon. SCIB said we could leave, but I figured you might want to wait around and find out what's in the pictures."

"I do. Thanks."

"Come on." He put his arm around her and guided her down the street toward the café. "I could eat a horse."

"Or a moose." They laughed, but weren't laughing an hour later when Joe's friend, the sergeant, slid alongside her into the booth at the café.

"Well?" Joe said.

"You guessed it. There were nearly a hundred photos, snapped automatically at thirty-second intervals over a period of about an hour."

"A hundred?"

"Professional film," Wendy explained. "Photographers can hand roll as many exposures as they want onto one roll." The moose burger congealed in her stomach. "And?"

"Ehrenberg was murdered. Carson showed up with one of his cronies and the kid went wild. The snapshots show him finding the video camera and trying to destroy the tape. Carson got a little carried away and hurt him. They probably thought the kid was gonna talk. Carson held a gun to his head and forced him to snort what had to be an ounce of Barrett's nose candy."

"Enough to kill," Joe said.

"You got it."

Wendy felt sick. "Poor Billy."

"Those New York detectives are good," the sergeant said. "Already collared the loan shark and his 'client'."

The "private collector", Wendy thought. "His poor parents."

"Billy's?" Joe said.

She nodded.

"I can relate."

The sergeant rose and clamped a hand on Joe's shoulder. "A little too close to home, isn't it?"

Wendy realized that the sergeant had probably known Cat.

"Yes and no," Joe said, surprising her. "Billy Ehrenberg didn't know what he was getting into. Cat did."

"I'm so sorry." Wendy slid her hand across the table. To her relief, Joe took it. "I didn't want you dragged into all this."

"Wouldn't have mattered," the sergeant said on his way out. "When Peterson wants to get involved, he gets involved. Am I right?"

She met Joe's steady gaze. "Too right."

They were quiet on the long drive back to the station.

Stan and Barb had dropped by the café before they'd left, and Wendy had asked if she could stay with them that night. She'd argued that it would be easier for her to retrieve her SUV from Retreat rather than the station, then get an early start into Anchorage to catch her flight back to New York.

Joe had put his foot down, and after a tense minute during which Barb and Stan had remained judiciously silent, Wendy had agreed to return to the station with him for the night.

He'd already made arrangements with the State Troopers to deliver her rental there the next day. To his surprise, it was already there waiting, the keys stuffed in an envelope in his mailbox, when they pulled into the driveway a little after ten.

Clouds obscured the last remnants of a late-summer sunset, but it was still light enough to see.

"You'll sleep better here," he said, grabbing the keys and her suitcase and ushering her to the front door. "It's quieter."

She shot him a look. "Retreat's not exactly a noisy metropolis."

He shrugged, aware of the fact that he didn't have one good excuse to give her for staying the night with him, except that he wanted her to. But he hadn't come right out and said that.

It was cold inside, and after he got the lights on and checked his phone messages—mercifully, there were none—he built a fire.

Wendy peeled off her jacket, shucked her boots and went into the kitchen. He heard her clearing up the mess they'd left earlier. Like their time together in the reserve, they moved almost unconsciously into an easy division of labor that felt good to him, natural. It was the kind of pattern couples develop after being together a long time.

He'd never thought of himself as part of a couple, certainly not in the past year, during which time he'd lived like a monk. Even before his sister died, he hadn't had any serious long-term relationships. It had never been a priority with him. Maybe he'd just never met the right woman.

As Wendy breezed into the room, wiping her wet hands on an old sweatshirt of his she'd chosen to put on earlier that day, he recalled her excitement at seeing the log house in the woods above Retreat, and knew he *had* met her.

"What is it?" she said.

"Nothing." He chucked another log on the fire and walked over to where she was standing.

"That's not a 'nothing' kind of look."

"No, you're right. It isn't." He took the dish towel out of her hand and tossed it on the desk. "My wanting you to stay tonight had nothing to do with anything except…I wanted you to stay."

"I know." Her eyes slayed him, innocent and sultry, and impossibly blue.

He placed his hands on her waist, and hers went

naturally to his biceps. He backed her into the hall, slowly, turning off lights as he went. He gave her plenty of time to resist, but she didn't.

"That night in the reserve, you'd just been through hell. You needed somebody, and I happened to be there. I wanted you then, and I want you now."

"Joe, I—"

"Let me finish." He stopped just short of his bedroom, easing her up against the door frame. "You needed me, but tonight I want you to want me. And if you don't, well…"

"I do." She slid her arms around his neck. "I do want you." And then she kissed him.

Chapter 16

Wendy knew she'd crossed the line, but couldn't stop herself. Making love to Joe tonight would make what she had to do tomorrow even harder. There was still time to be rational, to ease herself out of his embrace and revisit the reasons why she was all wrong for him, and he for her.

But she couldn't. She just couldn't. His heat, his tongue in her mouth, his hands on her body infused her with more than desire. She'd never felt this way about any man. She hadn't even thought it possible.

Without preamble, Joe scooped her into his arms and carried her to his bed. Moonlight splashed through the undraped windows, bathing the room in alternating bands of shadow and light. His eyes glittered as he eased her down onto the rumpled sheets and began to undress her.

They didn't speak, just looked at each other, touched, kissed tenderly as she worked the buttons of his shirt and he slid her jeans over her hips. When they were naked, he moved on top of her and kissed her with an urgency she shared. Instinctively, she spread her legs and wrapped them snugly around his hips, cradling him in her heat. His shaft throbbed like a velvet hammer against her.

"Not yet," he whispered against her lips, adjusting his position so she could no longer feel his need. With excruciating control, he embarked on a journey of gentle kisses trailed over her throat, across the sensitive skin of her shoulders to her breasts.

"Oh, Joe." She closed her eyes and arched into him as he playfully toyed with her nipples, alternately sucking and biting them, each in turn. They glistened with his saliva. He looked at her with a hunger she'd seen in him before—the day they'd met and again that night in the cabin.

Before she could catch her breath, he moved lower, her hands in his hair, tasting his way across her stomach, dipping his tongue briefly into her belly button before nuzzling the triangle of hair protecting her sex.

She nearly came off the bed.

"Easy." He held her down, kissed the insides of her thighs, forcing them apart as he used his tongue on her. He was gentle but unrelenting. The buildup was almost painful. Her climax was swift and powerful, taking her by surprise. She lost herself in it, in him, only peripherally aware that she cried his name, twining her fingers in his hair.

A heartbeat later he was on top of her. "I...I don't have any condoms." In the moonlight he looked like a wild animal, his hair hanging in his eyes, his face a pearly fusion of desire and need.

"I don't care," she heard herself whisper, her body boneless, her mind adrift in his eyes.

And then he was inside her.

Her breath caught. She came apart when he began thrusting, more violently this time, her nails digging into his biceps, her legs wrapped so tightly around him it was a miracle he could move.

She went with it, forcing herself to hold his gaze, deliberately letting him see her, what he was doing to her, what she felt for him but could not describe.

"I love you," he whispered, stunning her, and went with her over the edge.

Afterward he held her for a long time, silent, his body a warm harbor cradling hers. She drifted as he stroked her thigh, nuzzled her hair, peppered her earlobe with tiny kisses.

"Stay with me," he said. "Don't go back."

"You know I have to."

"Then let me go with you."

She turned in his arms and looked up at him. "No, Joe. I have to do this on my own."

"Do what? Give a couple of depositions, sit in a police station for hours with a bunch of detectives while they rehash the details."

"I need to talk to Vivian, even if I don't go to Blake's funeral." She hadn't decided about that yet. "I have to develop the caribou photos and deliver them to the magazine. Then there are my parents." She cringed, thinking about her father's reaction to all this. "I need to call them, explain. Then I have to figure out what to do with my apartment." She'd never be able to afford the Upper West Side flat on the salary the magazine had offered her.

"There are a million things." The most important of which was getting her head screwed on straight, and she couldn't do that here with him.

"I can help you. I want to help you. I love you, damn it! Didn't you hear me?"

She launched herself off the bed, and he instantly pulled her back down. She fought him, but he rolled on top of her, pinning her with his weight.

"No! Let go of me! Don't you get it?"

He kissed her, hard. "I get that I want you in my life."

She stopped struggling, went limp in his arms. "But first I have to straighten out *my* life. I've made mistakes, and some really bad decisions that have landed me in trouble. Three people are dead."

"None of that's your fault."

"Not directly, but I'm involved. This isn't something you can just fix for me, Joe, no matter how badly you want to. I have to take care of this on my own."

He rolled off her, onto his side, pulling her with him. "Is that such a bad thing, me wanting to fix it?"

"Yes, in this case. Yes, because of where I am in my life and where you are in yours."

"I'm here," he said. "I'm just here, and I want you here with me."

She closed her eyes and wondered what would happen if she simply gave in. She wanted to, more than anything, and that scared her more than her feelings for him and his for her, which she feared were confused.

"Loving someone isn't the same thing as keeping them safe, Joe, hidden away in the middle of nowhere where you think you can protect them from the world.''

She hadn't wanted to spell it out, but he'd left her no choice. He looked at her, and she knew from the pain in his eyes that her words had hit home.

''Let's not talk about it anymore.'' She brushed a stray hank of hair out of his eyes and kissed him gently on the mouth.

His arms slid around her, but he didn't respond. She kissed him again, more urgently this time, and his tongue mated with hers. The feeling was bittersweet. His touch, when he ran his hand along the length of her body, was tentative, as if they were starting over.

They were, in a way. The past few days they'd managed to strip each other's emotions raw. He'd let her inside his head and his heart, and she was powerless, now, to keep him out of hers.

They made love, slowly this time, his gaze pinned on hers, and again she did not look away. This time she knew what she felt for him.

This time she knew it was love.

Sometime before dawn Joe awoke to the sputter of an engine turning over in the driveway. Wendy's SUV. The empty space next to him in bed where she'd slept was still warm.

He willed himself to not go after her, forced himself to lie there, twisted in sheets that smelled of her and of their lovemaking, until he heard the Explorer slip into gear and the spray of gravel under the tires as she drove away.

Three days later, standing beside his sister's grave, watching the sun rise over an icy morning, Joe knew

Wendy was right. He was living out at the station, alone, miles from anywhere and anyone, for a reason.

He knew she thought he was hiding, too, protecting himself the same way he'd wanted to protect her. Maybe there was some truth to that, maybe he'd made himself believe he liked living the way he did. But it wasn't the real reason he'd stepped down from his job at the department managing local habitat and restoration projects, and had sequestered himself away in the reserve.

He was punishing himself.

As he knelt and laid the small bouquet of flowers on Cat's grave, he faced the fact that he'd been punishing himself for years—not for his mistakes, but for his sister's. Her death had been the catalyst that had finally driven him over the edge.

He knew now that no amount of penance in the world would bring her back, nor would it ever absolve his guilt, because that guilt was grossly misplaced.

He'd made himself responsible for her actions, while, in fact, he wasn't. He hadn't been her keeper, though he'd tried to be. He'd simply been her brother. And as a whole, when he looked back on their years together, he thought he'd been a damned good one.

"Rest easy, kid." He rose from the half-frozen ground and imagined what her response would be. "You, too, Joe," she'd have said.

On impulse, as he drove away from the small graveyard outside town, on his way back to the station, Joe turned off the road onto Elkhorn Drive. Steam wafted off the damp roof shingles of the house he'd built with his own hands as the sun, rising higher in the clear sky, struck it.

Once, he couldn't wait to move into it. It had been a long time since he'd thought about living here— more than a year—but he thought about it now. Standing on the wide covered porch last night with Wendy, watching as she'd run a hand along the rough-hewn timbers, he'd thought about living here with her.

She'd thought about it, too. He'd read it in her eyes and in her face when, together, hand in hand, they'd crossed the threshold and had gone inside.

It only took him a few minutes to get the heat going and prime the well. Though the house had been vacant since he'd finished it last summer, had weathered one hard winter and a wet spring, everything worked just fine. It ought to. The place was new.

Walking across the expanse of hand-laid hardwood flooring in the great room, he looked at the stone fireplace and pictured Wendy's wildlife photos flanking it. Hell, he could see a whole wall of them.

Opening the door to the storage area under the stairs, he envisioned it as her darkroom. He thought about what it would be like to come home from work each day and find her here.

"Yeah," he said to himself, walking from room to room, imagining feminine touches, picturing Wendy sitting at the kitchen table or curled up in bed.

His bed. Their bed.

By the time he slammed on the brakes in the gravel parking lot of the Department of Fish and

Game offices in town, he was imagining all kinds of things. Wonderful things, impossible things.

"Possible," he told himself, and bounded up the stairs into the building.

It was Sunday, but the lights were on in the office, the door unlocked. He jerked it open and raced down the hall toward the coffee room.

"Hey!" a voice called from one of the offices as he passed. He glanced back, not breaking his stride, and saw Barb's springy curls as she poked her head out of her office. A pair of reading glasses, perched low on her nose, accentuated her raised brows. "What's up?"

"Everything," he said, and turned the corner into the coffee room, Barb on his heels. His gaze zeroed in on the bulletin board on the wall, plastered haphazardly with official department memorandums.

He ripped them off the board, one by one, until he got to the one he wanted—the year-old posting for the job the department had never refilled. His job.

"Oh, my God." Barb watched, her eyes big brown saucers, as he folded the paper and stuffed it into his pocket. "You're coming back!"

"Yeah. Get ready." Turning on his heel, he retraced his steps down the corridor to the corner office that had once been his.

"This is great! Stan's gonna have kittens!"

"Tell him not to have them yet," he said, and grabbed the phone. He hitched a hip on the side of his old desk and punched in numbers. It felt good, damned good. He'd been away far too long and hadn't realized how much he'd missed it.

"Are you calling the boss? He refused to hire anyone else, you know. He said you'd come back when you were ready. That it was only a matter of time before—''

"Reservations," he said into the receiver.

Barb's mouth dropped open. "You're doing it! You're going after her, aren't you?"

He shot her a pithy look, then turned his attention to the phone call. "Yeah, one way—for now. Anchorage to New York."

Chapter 17

The food at her favorite SoHo bistro seemed bland and tasteless. Wendy toyed with chunks of seared ahi and the vinaigrette-dressed arugula on her plate, and thought about the deluxe moose burger she and Joe had shared at the little café in Retreat.

"You're a million miles away. What gives?" Her college friend and soon-to-be editor, Crystal, arched a perfectly plucked brow at her.

"I don't know. I just can't stop thinking about it."

She'd arrived in New York after midnight last Thursday and had spent most of Friday and half of Saturday with the police. The authorities had reopened Billy Ehrenberg's case, now that the truth was known, and fortunately for her she hadn't been charged with anything more serious than stupidity, and was free to go.

On Saturday afternoon she'd attended Blake's funeral, a huge, elegant affair. Despite the ugly truth of his dealings with mob loan sharks and his culpability in Billy Ehrenberg's death—which the tabloids had publicized the second they'd found out—everyone who was anyone in the business had been there.

She'd spent a little time afterward with Vivian Barrett, who, to Wendy's surprise, seemed in amazingly good spirits, almost as if she was relieved that Blake was out of her life. Wendy shuddered, not wanting to think about what that said about their marriage.

Yesterday, Sunday, she'd spent the entire day in the lab at *Wilderness Unlimited* headquarters around the corner from where she and Crystal were having lunch. The caribou photos were everything she'd hoped they'd be, and the editorial director of the magazine had come through on the spot with the promised offer of permanent employment.

Through it all she'd had a hard time focusing on anything or anyone except Joe. Five days and he hadn't called her—not that she'd left him her phone number. She reminded herself that she hadn't called him, either.

She'd told him she needed to sort things out on her own, in her own time. Alone, without him. He'd respected that choice, even though she knew it went against his nature, and for that she loved him.

"Hello-o-o." Crystal waved a hand in front of her face. Wendy snapped to attention. "You mean you can't stop thinking about *him.* Joe Forest Ranger."

"Game warden," she said. "And you're right. I can't."

Crystal pushed her plate aside and flipped open the portfolio of proofs Wendy had brought with her to their luncheon. Crystal blew by the caribou photos and went right to the last page. A photo of Joe, his face half in shadow, half in light, stared up at them.

"Wow." Crystal ran a bright-red fingernail over the proof and sighed. "I can see why. He's gorgeous." She tilted her head and examined the composition. "In an unkempt, rugged sort of way, of course."

"We'd hiked nearly forty miles in bad weather when I took that. Of course he's...rugged looking."

"Mmm, nice. He'd make a great model."

"Don't even think about it." That was the last thing Joe Peterson would ever do.

Crystal closed the portfolio and handed it back to her. "You're sure about *WU?* That this is what you want?"

"I'm sure."

"I've had calls from some of your friends at *Esquire* and *GQ,*" Crystal said. "They want you."

She recalled the catered party Vivian Barrett had thrown after Blake's funeral. Wendy had received three offers of work back in fashion photography, the industry that barely six weeks ago had blackballed her. The sensationalized publicity around the murders was now perceived to be some kind of macabre benefit.

Wendy shook her head. "I don't know. It's just not *me* anymore."

"It never was, kiddo." Crystal eyed Wendy's short fingernails, her simple khaki pants and forest-green tank top. "You were never really a New Yorker."

She regarded Crystal's chic black dress, impeccable makeup and gaudy jewelry. "How on earth did you ever end up at a wildlife magazine?'' Crystal was the stereotypical hip New Yorker.

"Oh, I don't know. It's different. Not for you, though. For you it seems like home.''

Home.

She sighed, recalling the log house in Retreat, remembering Joe kissing her in the storage area under the stairs, and their lovemaking the night before she left him. "I don't know where that is anymore.''

"You know some of our staff photographers live in the field.''

"What do you mean?''

"You know what I mean. They live where they work. Rather than traveling all the time, they're assigned to a region and live there. In the case of Alaska, it would just be the state.''

Wendy had already thought of that, the day she left Joe's station before dawn.

"Think about it,'' Crystal said. "*WU* doesn't have anyone living in Alaska right now. It could work.''

Not wanting to think about it, she grabbed the bill when the waiter brought it and tried to calculate the tip in her head. She couldn't. Her brain was buzzing.

"This is on the magazine.'' Crystal snatched the bill out of her hand and set it on the table along with a crisp fifty-dollar bill. "I've got to get back.''

"Yeah. Me, too.'' Movers were coming tomorrow. Wendy had to be out of her apartment by the end of the week. She wasn't sure where she was going yet, but knew she couldn't afford to keep the pricey Upper West Side flat on the salary the wildlife magazine promised to pay her.

"You okay?''

She smiled at her friend. Crystal had known her

since their first day at college, long before she'd taken the name Willa. It seemed so foreign to her now, as if she'd never used the pseudonym.

"Yeah," she said. "I'm okay."

"You're in love with him."

"What?" She shook her head and rose from the hard-backed restaurant chair. "No. It's just…"

"Love." Crystal slung an arm around her, and they walked out together into the muggy lunchtime bustle of Spring Street. "I know it when I see it, and you've got it, kiddo. You've got it bad."

They parted at the corner, promising to talk tomorrow, then Wendy caught a cab back to her apartment. The traffic was bad, the heat stifling, and on the way she thought about what Crystal had said.

Manhattan didn't seem the same to her anymore. She used to love the excitement, the diversity. Now it just seemed drab and hot—ungodly hot. What she wouldn't give for a breath of cool Alaskan air. She supposed she'd have the opportunity to experience it again at some point. A magazine like *Wilderness Unlimited* did lots of photo essays there, nearly one a month. Plenty, she thought, to keep a full-time photographer busy. Or even a part-time photographer— one with a husband and kids.

Oh, stop it!

After she paid the cabbie and jogged up the two flights of stairs to her apartment, the first thing she noticed when she opened the door was the message machine blinking at her. That, and the phone, were the few remaining things she hadn't packed. As she snaked through stacks of moving boxes, her pulse began to quicken.

Maybe Joe had called.

She punched the play button and spent the next few minutes listening to the pleas of two fashion photography houses and three more magazines that wanted her to work for them. She couldn't even muster up a smile, not one shred of excitement. She should at least be happy her professional reputation had been restored.

Erasing the messages, she kicked her shoes off and plopped down on her bed, wondering what Joe was doing right now, four thousand miles away.

The phone rang four more times that afternoon and evening. Four more job offers. Wendy turned them all down. She unplugged the message machine and put it in a half-packed box. She was exhausted but couldn't sleep, still hungry but couldn't eat.

At eleven-thirty that night, the phone rang again. This time she ripped it out of the wall.

Joe tried the number again and let it ring a couple of dozen times before he gave up, replacing the sticky receiver of the pay phone and stepping out of the booth onto Seventy-Second Street.

He'd snagged Wendy's phone number from directory assistance, but her address was unlisted, and he had no idea where she lived except that it was somewhere in Manhattan's Upper West Side.

For all he knew, he could be standing right in front of her building. He half thought about checking the names on the long metal rows of doorbells and mailboxes some of the older buildings sported.

"Give it up for tonight," he said to himself.

He knew enough about the city from the week he'd spent here last year after Cat's death, to know where things were and how to get around. It had taken him all day to get here from Anchorage, and he was exhausted. Not from the travel, but because he hadn't slept the night before. Christ, he hadn't had a decent night's sleep since Wendy left.

He needed sleep now, desperately. Before hopping a cab back to the modest hotel that had been recommended to him by one of those Information people at the airport, he plucked a scrap of paper out of his pocket and fished around for more change.

He still had the home phone number of Wendy's editor. He remembered Wendy had told him the woman was a night owl, so he didn't hesitate to make the call. Again, there was no answer.

"Damn!"

He didn't like giving up, but it was nearly midnight on a Monday, and finally he had to concede that there was no way to find Wendy's address until tomorrow.

Now that he was here, had made the decision to come after her, he couldn't wait to see her, hold her, tell her again that he loved her. But he would have to wait—one more night.

Frustrated, he caught a cab to his hotel.

Joe was standing outside the locked door of *Wilderness Unlimited* headquarters in SoHo, when the receptionist arrived at work the next day at eight-thirty.

"I'm looking for Wendy Walters," he said, following the young woman into the suite of offices that occupied the lower floor of what once must have been a warehouse.

"Uh, she's new, right?"

"Yeah. Just started. She's a photographer." He

stood at the receptionist's desk and drummed his knuckles on the wood as she leisurely checked her makeup, then stashed her purse in a drawer. "Maybe you could just give me her address."

"Oh." The receptionist frowned at him, noting for the first time his rumpled-looking clothes. He'd left Alaska in a hurry and hadn't packed more than an extra shirt and his shaving kit. "I couldn't do that even if I knew it."

"Why not?"

She looked at him with suspicion, as if she thought he might be a serial killer or a kook. "Because I just couldn't. I could get fired if—"

"Well, well, well," a feminine voice quipped from the reception area behind them. Joe turned to see a tall, smartly dressed woman breeze into the office. She was carrying two cups of coffee in foam containers and a portfolio the size of a small state. "You're *him*."

"Him who?" Joe absently accepted the foam cup she thrust in his direction.

"Joe Peterson, right? Crystal Chalmers, Wendy's editor."

He was so stunned that she knew him, he just stood there like an idiot when she offered him her elegantly manicured hand.

"Sorry, hon," she said to the receptionist, ignoring his bad manners. "You'll have to get your own latte this morning. This guy looks like he needs it more than you do."

Without waiting for either of them to respond, Crystal started down the hall. Joe followed her. Her office was huge, the walls decorated with framed photographs of wildlife and scenery.

"Have a seat." She dropped the portfolio on her desk and popped the lid off her coffee. Latte, Joe reminded himself, and did as she asked him, easing into the comfortable guest chair in front of her desk.

He sipped at the hot drink. "Thanks."

"My pleasure. Now, Joe Peterson, game warden and self-appointed protector of the hottest photographer in town, I suppose you're here to find Wendy."

His head was spinning. "How do you know me?"

She arched a brow at him. "Come on. You barrel in here at the crack of dawn, looking as if you hadn't had a wink of sleep in days—mind you, Wendy looked like that, too, when I saw her yesterday—and practically maul our receptionist trying to get your girlfriend's address. Who else could you possibly be?"

"She's not my girlfriend. She's—"

"Well, she ought to be. Looks to me like she ought to be more than that. But that's another story. Right now I suspect you just want to find her."

"Yeah, I do. But how—"

"Calm down. I'm not telepathic or anything. I saw some photos of you. Nice shots, too." She smiled at him.

He remembered that Wendy had taken some photographs of him when they were in the reserve. He also remembered blowing his stack at her for taking them. That was before he knew her, before he loved her. It was barely a couple of weeks ago but seemed like a lifetime.

He'd changed a lot in the past two weeks and envisioned even more changes in his life before he was done. Good ones, and they all started today.

"Before I give you her address, I'd like you to see something."

"What?"

Crystal opened the portfolio. "Some eight-by-tens of the caribou shots Wendy brought back from Alaska. Here." She handed him the portfolio. "Take a look."

Joe studied the photographs, awed. Wendy had managed to capture on film what so many had missed over the years—the raw emotion of the setting, the power and majesty of the animals he'd worked with all his years in the department.

"These are wonderful."

"Wendy's a powerhouse. Real talent."

"And guts," he said, remembering how she'd crawled out onto that ledge to take the photos.

"That, too. But she's not used to going with it— her gut, I mean. She might need a little…coaxing." Crystal pulled a fountain pen out of her desk drawer and scribbled something on a piece of paper. "Here's her address," she said, and handed it to him. "Better hurry. She's moving today."

"Moving?" His stomach did a slow roll. "Where?"

Crystal shrugged. "I don't know. That's up to her—and you."

The movers arrived early. Wendy slept late. She'd barely had time to throw on some clothes and grab a coffee before they started moving furniture out of her apartment.

The truck was down on the street. She stood at the window, sipping the brew, watching as three burly guys hefted her sofa onto the tailgate. It hadn't taken them long, mostly because she didn't have that much stuff.

She'd spent the majority of the past seven years working, and hadn't had time to accumulate much in the way of belongings. Which was a good thing, she thought, as she walked over to the remaining boxes that were stacked beside her small galley kitchen, waiting to be loaded. It made moving easier.

Yesterday she'd found a share rental in SoHo, not far from the *Wilderness Unlimited* office. Also not far from three of the top fashion photography houses who'd offered her jobs in the past forty-eight hours.

She plucked a couple of formal offers that had arrived a few minutes ago by courier off the kitchen counter and looked at them. She'd be a fool not to take one of them. Even Crystal had said as much at their lunch yesterday. The money was outrageous.

It was as if she'd become a hot property overnight, and for no apparent reason. There was so much competition between top photographers, it was almost as if, once one of them had made her an offer, others felt compelled to do the same, upping the ante. Kind of like the "herd instinct" of the stock market. Once one person buys, everybody starts to buy.

Not that she wasn't talented and didn't deserve it. She was. That's what she'd come to realize the past month and a half, and what had been reinforced in Alaska the past few weeks. She was talented and capable and could make of her life whatever she wanted.

The question is…what do I want?

A half-packed box sat open on the counter, the edges of a couple of black-and-white eight-by-tens sticking out of the top. Wendy's chest tightened as she pulled them from the box.

They were the pictures she'd taken of Joe. On Sunday, in *WU*'s lab, she'd developed and printed them along with the caribou photos. Crystal hadn't seen these two particular shots. Wendy hadn't wanted anyone to see them. They were personal.

Her back against the fridge, she slid to the floor and sat cross-legged, looking at them. They were beautiful. He was beautiful. The play of darkness and light on the bronzed muscles of his back. The hard curve of his biceps, the definition in his hand—all against a backdrop of tangled foliage and dead summer wildflowers.

But it wasn't his body that moved her, so much as his face, his expression—a calm fusion of pain and control, hope and something she couldn't quite put her finger on. In one shot he was looking right at her.

Studying it made her remember.

And she didn't want to remember. Or did she?

In the wildlife reserve, in an unrelenting barrage of life-threatening situations, he'd afforded her the freedom to make her own choices, decisions that had affected them both.

He'd been a partner to her.

"A *partner*," she said out loud.

He'd told her he loved her. He'd opened himself to her, had shared with her his pain and his dreams. She thought about the log house and what he must have been like when he'd built it—full of hope, excitement, goals for the future.

A future he wanted to share with her.

"Where to, lady? We gotta roll." The moving man's booming voice made her jump.

"Uh, I don't know." Her head spinning, she scrambled to her feet and, with shaking hands, stuffed the photos back in the box. "G-give me a minute."

"You *don't know?*" His bushy brows shot skyward. "Geez, talk about last-minute decisions, huh?"

"Uh, yeah." That's exactly what it was, she thought, as she rifled through the box. A last-minute decision. A *crazy* decision.

She hunted through the box until she found the slim-line telephone she'd just packed. It only took her a second to plug it back into the wall and punch in the numbers for directory assistance.

"So, ya decided yet?" The moving man crowded her with his clipboard, a pen poised between beefy fingers waiting to jot down an address.

"Uh, no. Yes, I mean." She asked the operator to wait, then turned to him. "Storage. You have a storage facility, right?"

"Well, yeah, but—"

"Just take everything there. I'll call you in a few days with an address."

"Sheesh." He jammed the pen behind his ear and looked at her as if she was nuts.

She *was* nuts, she realized.

"It's gonna cost ya. Storage ain't cheap."

"That's okay. Just do it."

He shrugged at her. "Okay, lady, you got it." He grabbed another box and started downstairs.

"Wait!" she called after him. "Hail me a cab, will you? I'll be right down." She turned her attention back to the operator, who had held so long he was about to disconnect. "Wait, don't hang up! I'm here."

A huffy sound preceded his annoyed, almost flippant demand. "What listing please?"

She took a breath, then took the plunge. "Alaska Airlines. Reservations."

Chapter 18

Traffic was a nightmare. On the street ahead there was an accident. Joe swore as the cab he was in screeched to a halt, trapped between a fire truck and an ambulance.

"Can't you get around it?"

The cab driver shrugged. "Maybe. How bad do you want me to try?"

"Bad," he said, and shoved another twenty at him through the hole in the Plexiglas partition.

"Hang on, then." The driver jumped the curb on the opposite side of the street from the accident, and a minute later they were free.

They turned onto Central Park West, and the driver floored it. Joe stared blankly at the scrap of paper Crystal had given him with Wendy's address scrawled on it. What was he going to say to her? That he just happened to be in town?

He sat back against the duct-taped vinyl seat and

rubbed his eyes. It was cards-on-the-table time. She'd had five days, hell, it was six days now, to sort things out. Granted, that wasn't a lot of time, but it was all the time he could stand apart from her, not knowing.

"How much farther?" he asked the driver.

"Not far."

They flew past the Museum of Natural History, and a few streets later the driver hung a left. Wendy's street. Thank God! It was jammed with cars and taxis, delivery trucks and pedestrians snaking in and out of the bumper-to-bumper traffic.

He looked for street numbers. One block, two. Couldn't they go any faster? He was tempted to get out of the cab and walk. Run. His hands were sweating. Just as he contemplated doing exactly that, he realized her building was just ahead. His gut tightened.

The street was choked with vehicles. A moving truck blocked traffic on the right-hand side. The ramp was still down, and he watched as a couple of guys pitched boxes onto the bed like they were softballs.

Better hurry. She's moving today.

Crystal's words hit him like a brick. The moving truck was Wendy's. She was still there! Joe flipped another ten at the driver and scrambled out of the cab. Sprinting up the street, he looked for her face amidst the menagerie of pedestrians in motion. Didn't see her.

Just as he reached the truck, a taxi pulled out from the curb and almost hit him as it swerved into traffic. "Son of a bitch!" He shot a murderous look at the driver, who casually shrugged.

"Apartment 2B?" he yelled to one of the movers.

"This building?" He pointed to the three-story brownstone sporting Wendy's street address.

"Yeah." The mover pitched another box into the truck.

Joe raced up the steps of the brownstone to the second floor. Wendy's apartment door stood open. He pulled up short and worked to catch his breath.

"Okay. Get a grip, Peterson." You're not going to make demands, you're simply going to ask her. Straight out.

He walked calmly down the hall, forcing himself to go slow, then stepped into the apartment.

It was empty.

From his vantage point in the kitchen, he could see the entire space—living area, bedroom and a couple of open closets. She wasn't there.

The bathroom door opened, the sound of the toilet flushing in the background, and Joe's stomach did a slow roll. He exhaled when he saw it was just one of the movers, a big beefy guy with a clipboard who was zipping up his fly.

"Where is she?" Joe said to him. "Wendy Walters, is she still here?"

"Nope." The mover took a final look around the empty apartment and checked a box on the form clipped to his board. "Caught a cab somewhere, 'bout a minute ago."

Joe swore. "What's her forwarding address?"

The moving man looked up from his clipboard. "Didn't give one. Her stuff's going to storage."

"Son of a—" He spotted a couple of courier service envelopes on the kitchen counter. Two letters lay next to them. He picked one up.

It was a job offer, addressed to Wendy, from an

outfit he'd heard his sister mention once. He didn't know squat about fashion photography, but he knew enough from looking at the salary they'd offered her that it was a damned good opportunity. The second offer was even higher.

"Come on, buddy, I gotta lock this place up." The moving man waited for him at the door. "Property management outfit's waitin' for the keys."

Joe handed him the letters. "She must've forgotten these."

"I'll stuff 'em in with her paperwork. Let's go."

Down on the street Joe walked aimlessly for blocks, alternately thinking about how he could find her and what an idiot he was for coming here in the first place.

It occurred to him that she might not want to be found.

He thought about calling Crystal Chalmers at the magazine. She was Wendy's friend and would know how to reach her. He also thought about getting drunk. It was only ten in the morning. Still, the idea appealed to him.

In the end he settled for a beer at the airport while he waited to board his afternoon flight back to Anchorage.

Wendy parked her rental in the gravel driveway and used the set of keys she knew Joe kept under a rock to open the door to his station. His pickup wasn't in the driveway, so she knew he wasn't there.

The first thing she noticed when she switched on the lamp in the front room was that the place was a mess. Papers were scattered across his office desk. The red light on his message machine blinked impatiently, indicating four messages. Two of them were hers.

She'd called him once from Kennedy that morning before boarding her flight, and again on the ground in Anchorage after she'd picked up her rental. Both times he either hadn't been home or hadn't wanted to take her call.

At first she'd feared the latter, but from the looks of the place, she suspected he hadn't been home. *Hasn't* been home in a few days, she thought, noticing the half-eaten cheese sandwich sitting on a napkin on the desk. The bread was hard as rock, the cheese desiccated.

"Joe?" she called, on the off chance she might be wrong. She wasn't.

Clothes were strewn across the hardwood floor from the front room to the bedroom. She picked them up as she moved down the hall, pausing in the bathroom to turn off the dripping shower and again in the bedroom where a couple of empty suitcases had been pulled down from the open closet.

The naked overhead bulb was still burning. As she switched it off, she pieced together what had gone on. He'd undressed, showered, then dressed again, and then had packed to go somewhere—all in a big hurry.

The question was...where had he gone and when would he be back?

She'd had hours on the flight from New York and the long drive from Anchorage to think about all the things she wanted to say to him when she got here. But now her mind was muddled. It was after midnight and she was bone tired, and all she wanted was for him to come home so she could hold him, kiss him, fall asleep in his arms.

She changed out of her traveling clothes into some leggings and one of his old sweatshirts. After managing to get a nice fire going in the fireplace to warm the place up, she went around the house turning off the lights she'd turned on when she'd arrived.

On his desk she glanced at the scattering of paperwork, and was stunned to see an application for transfer from his current job in the reserve to the more responsible position he'd once held. Underneath it was an equally surprising piece of paper—an order from the local telephone company to begin service at the house on Elkhorn Drive.

Joe Peterson was taking his life back.

Wendy smiled.

Her joy turned to nervous excitement as she heard the unmistakable approach of a vehicle, tires spinning on gravel as a truck pulled into the driveway. Joe's truck.

She backed to the sofa, leaned against it for support and waited, her stomach fluttering as his footfalls sounded on the creaky boards of the deck outside, as his key turned in the lock.

The door opened, and the moment Joe saw her he stopped, shock registering on his face.

''Joe,'' she said.

''Wendy.''

She wanted to run to him, to blurt out everything she felt, all that she hoped for, before he had a chance to react, but her body failed her. Her feet were like lead, glued to the floor. Her throat closed and her chest tightened. She found herself struggling just to breathe.

"Wendy," he said again, and dropped what he was carrying—some kind of overnight bag—on the floor.

She watched, unable to move, as he closed the distance between them in three strides. Firelight caught in his eyes and danced there as he looked at her, his face bathed in gold, reminding her of the first night they'd made love. What she read in his expression finally broke the spell.

"Joe!" She threw her arms around him, and he lifted her off her feet. They kissed, wildly, frantically, his hands moving over her in a possessive frenzy that she, too, felt. "Oh, Joe!" She lost herself in his scent, the feel of his arms around her, his kisses, the beat of his heart against her chest.

"What are you doing here?" He scooped her into his arms, moved around the sofa and sat down with her in his lap. "I can't believe it."

They looked at each other for a long tender minute, silent, touching—his thumb brushing her lips, her fingertip tracing the line of his jaw—as if they were blind lovers reading each other's faces for the first time.

"I needed to see you," she said at last.

"I needed to see you, too." His arms moved solidly around her and held her close to him. "That's where I was, where I went, I mean. To see you. I had no idea—"

"What?" Her breath caught when she glanced at the airline ticket stub sticking out of his shirt pocket. "You came to see me? In *New York?*"

"Yeah. Uh, two days ago. At least I think it was two days ago. What day is this?"

"I don't know. Wednesday. No, Tuesday." She looked at him, thunderstruck.

"Are you angry that I came after you?"

"No." She brushed his hair away from his face so she could see his eyes better. Tiny bonfires reflected back at her, heating her blood.

"It wasn't because I thought you couldn't handle things on your own. I knew you could, and wanted to give you a few days to get your feet on the ground." His expression turned serious. "Did you?"

"Yes." She filled him in on how the murder investigation had turned out, assuring him that it was behind her now, that she was free. She told him about Blake's funeral, how Vivian Barrett had adapted to her widow's status with an enthusiasm that was almost shocking.

Joe told her about his whirlwind trip to Manhattan. She was stunned to discover he'd gone to the magazine and had met Crystal. Not so stunned that her meddling friend had given him her home address.

"I—we must have missed each other." By hours, maybe even minutes, she thought. They'd even flown back to Anchorage on the same airline, but had taken different flights. "Why didn't you call me?"

"I did call you. Dozens of times, but—"

"It doesn't matter now." She quieted him with a kiss. "You're here."

"*You're* here," he said, his face alight with emotion. "Why?"

"Don't you know?" She snaked her arms around his neck.

"Tell me."

She wanted to tell him everything, a million

things—but only one thing was important. "I love you."

He looked at her, silent, his gaze pinned to hers. His arms tightened around her.

"I said I love you."

"I know." He grinned. "I just wanted to hear you say it again."

She thumped him.

They laughed, and then he kissed her, long and tenderly. She melted into him, and knew it was right. *He* was right for her, and *she* was right, but only with him. She realized that now. She also realized that her life didn't have to exist on a scale between control and being controlled, that love meant partnership.

Joe Peterson taught her that.

Suddenly he pulled back, cupping her face in his hands so he could see her. "I'm making some changes, Wendy."

"I know. The house in town, your job… I saw the papers on your desk."

"It's time I got a life again."

"Me, too."

His eyes clouded. "I saw some papers at your place, too."

"You mean my apartment? You were there?"

"For about a minute, while the movers were just finishing—long enough to see a couple of pretty good job offers."

She remembered she'd left them on the counter. "They weren't so good."

"No?" He looked at her, an unspoken question in his eyes.

"No."

He beamed her the most beautiful smile she'd ever seen. "So, what do you think? About the log house, I mean."

"The one in town? The one you built? I think it's a pretty big house for one guy."

"I was thinking that, too." He kissed her again, longer this time and more passionately, and she felt him grow hard beneath her.

"You might want a roommate." She nibbled mischievously at his ear. "Someone, say, in a related field."

"Like a wildlife photographer?"

"Exactly. But only a good one. Someone who works for a big magazine, who just landed a permanent assignment in Alaska."

"You're kidding? That's great!" He looked at her, joy shining in his face, but she waited, unable to breathe until she heard his answer. His smile faded. "But, no. I don't want a roommate."

Her stomach did a flip-flop. "You...don't?"

"There wouldn't be room."

"There wouldn't?"

"Nope. You see, I was thinking about getting married, having kids. The whole nine yards."

Wendy couldn't breathe. "You...were? Are?"

He nodded. "The only thing is, she hasn't said yes yet."

Her fingers dug into his shoulders involuntarily. "Well, um, maybe that's because you haven't told her you loved her—not for a few days, anyway."

He eased her off him and onto the soft cushions of the sofa and moved carefully on top of her. Firelight washed gold across his rugged features, flickered in his hazel eyes. "I love you, Wendy Walters. Marry me."

Her body ignited when he kissed her. "How many kids?" she breathed.

"I don't know. Four?"

"Four!"

"Three, then."

She gazed up at him and saw all the years of love and happiness they would share shining back at her in his eyes.

"Yes."

*   *   *   *   *

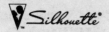

INTIMATE MOMENTS™

is proud to present a thrilling new miniseries by award-winning author

INGRID WEAVER

Elite warriors who live—and love— by their own code of honor.

Be swept into a world of romance, danger and international intrigue as elite Delta Force commandos risk their lives and their hearts in the name of justice—and true love!

Available in February 2003:

EYE OF THE BEHOLDER (IM #1204)

After putting his life on the line to rescue beautiful Glenna Hastings from the clutches of an evil drug lord and landing in a hidden jungle prison, can Master Sergeant Rafe Marek protect Glenna—from himself?

Continuing in April 2003:

SEVEN DAYS TO FOREVER (IM #1216)

Available at your favorite retail outlet.

If you enjoyed what you just read,
then we've got an offer you can't resist!

Take 2 bestselling love stories FREE!

Plus get a FREE surprise gift!

New York Times bestselling author

DEBBIE MACOMBER

weaves emotional tales of love and longing.

Here is the first
of her celebrated
NAVY series!

Dare Lindy risk her heart
on a man whose duty
would keep taking
him away from her?

*Available this February
wherever Silhouette books
are sold.*

#1201 ONE OF THESE NIGHTS—Justine Davis
Redstone, Incorporated

Ian Gamble was on the verge of a billion-dollar invention, and someone was willing to kill for it. To keep him safe, security agent Samantha Beckett went undercover and became his secret bodyguard. Samantha soon fell for the sexy scientist, but when her cover was blown, would she be able to repair the damage in time to save his life—and her heart?

#1202 THE CINDERELLA MISSION—Catherine Mann
Family Secrets

Millionaire CIA agent Ethan Williams had his mission: find a missing operative, and his new partner was none other than language specialist Kelly Taylor. As he watched his bookish friend transform herself into a sexy secret agent, Ethan faced long-buried feelings. He was willing to risk his own life for the job, but how could he live with risking Kelly's?

#1203 WILDER DAYS—Linda Winstead Jones

After years apart, DEA agent Del Wilder was reunited with his high school sweetheart, Victoria Lowell. A killer out for revenge was hunting them, and Del vowed to protect Victoria and her daughter—especially once he learned that he was the father. Would a sixteen-year-old secret ruin their chance for family? Or could love survive the second time around?

#1204 EYE OF THE BEHOLDER—Ingrid Weaver
Eagle Squadron

With a hijacker's gun to her throat, Glenna Hastings' only hope was wounded Delta Force Master Sergeant Rafe Marek. As they were held captive in a remote jungle compound, their fear exploded into passion. Afterward, Rafe desperately wanted to be with Glenna. But could he give her a bright future, or would he merely remind her of a dark, terrifying past?

#1205 BURIED SECRETS—Evelyn Vaughn

Haunted by his wife's mysterious death, ex-cop Zack Lorenzo was determined to defeat the black magic being practiced in the West Texas desert. And Sheriff Josephine James was determined to help him—whether she liked it or not. As they plunged into a world of sinister evil and true love, they realized they held the most powerful weapon of all....

#1206 WHO DO YOU TRUST?—Melissa James

Lissa Carroll loved Mitch McCluskey despite his mysterious ways. But when she was approached with evidence claiming he was a kidnapper, she wasn't sure what to believe. Searching for the truth, she learned that Mitch was actually an Australian spy. Now he was forced to bring her into his high-stakes world, or risk losing her love—or her life—forever....